'Where are we...

Zoe snapped h... ...
sarcastically. 'Oh, ...ack;
well I haven't been before so perhaps you'll
enlighten me as to what exactly I do need—an
asbestos body-stocking?'

'Why don't you just come in that delightfully
scented skin of yours? It served you well
enough three years ago.'

'Three years ago I was two years old; now I'm
five and a hundred years older.'

Dear Reader

Easter is upon us, and with it our thoughts turn to the meaning of Easter. For many, it's a time when Nature gives birth to all things, so what better way to begin a new season of love and romance than by reading some of the new authors whom we have recently introduced to our lists? Watch out for Helen Brooks, Jenny Cartwright, Liz Fielding, Sharon Kendrick and Catherine O'Connor—all of whom have books coming out this spring!

The Editor

Natalie Fox was born and brought up in London and has a daughter, two sons and two grandsons. Her husband, Ian, is a retired advertising executive, and they now live in a tiny Welsh village. Natalie is passionate about her three cats, two of them strays brought back from Spain where she lived for five years, and equally passionate about gardening and writing romance. Natalie says she took up writing because she absolutely *hates* going out to work!

Recent titles by the same author:

REVENGE
LOVE IN TORMENT
AN IMPERFECT AFFAIR

LOVE ON LOAN

BY
NATALIE FOX

MILLS & BOON LIMITED
ETON HOUSE   18-24 PARADISE ROAD
RICHMOND   SURREY   TW9 1SR

*First published in Great Britain 1993
by Mills & Boon Limited*

© Natalie Fox 1993

*Australian copyright 1993
Philippine copyright 1993
This edition 1993*

ISBN 0 263 77969 6

*Set in Times Roman 11 on 12 pt.
01-9304-48754 C*

Made and printed in Great Britain

CHAPTER ONE

'I BELIEVE I've already had the pleasure,' Franc Blakemore offered drily as he stretched out his hand to Zoe Marston.

Theodosius Koriakis missed the suggestive tone of Blakemore's voice as he made the introductions, but it struck Zoe deep into the fragile nest of her heart.

She clutched her small fists to her side, willing them to stay there. She couldn't touch this man, not again, not even for Theo who controlled her life.

Her heart recovered and steeled itself and she directed a transparent smile at the tall, dark, striking man in front of her, but she couldn't meet those smoke-grey eyes of his; after what had happened between them she hadn't enough nerve for that.

'That's what they all say,' she murmured, her voice oozing sarcasm, timed and delivered at the moment Theo's attention was diverted by the announcement of another guest at his lavish fiftieth birthday party. It wouldn't do for Theo to know they had already met at another of his gatherings three years previously.

Franc Blakemore soaked up her suggestive sarcasm with a controlled smile but a betraying pulse at his throat showed Zoe she had got to him, and that surprised her. She didn't think any woman was capable of getting to him, least of all herself.

'Zoe, keep Blakemore happy while I greet my other guests.'

'Yes, Zoe, keep Blakemore happy,' Franc echoed with a heavy drawl after Theo had left them alone on the marbled terrace of his Corinthian-columned fortress. It was Zoe's home too, and her place of employment—and, of late, prison. 'Just as you were ordered to do three years ago,' Frank added silkily, 'and very well you did it too.'

Zoe turned abruptly away from him. Her hands grasped the cool stone balustrade that separated the terrace from the pool and her deep brown eyes narrowed painfully at the remark. Her long jet hair streamed in the hot breeze and then fell around her bare shoulders, prickling her skin till she shivered. She'd known he was coming and thought she had prepared herself for facing him once again, but she was wrong about that.

'I...I wasn't *ordered* to do what I did, Mr Blakemore,' she attempted painfully, but realised the folly of her words immediately. She felt the heat rise from her throat to colour her smooth olive skin as he laughed softly behind her.

'You did it because you wanted to, eh?' He came and stood beside her, lifted her silky hair from her shoulders and tilted her chin towards him. 'Very becoming, a blushing whore—and one who actually enjoys her work.'

His words stung, his fingers on her heated flesh stung, the whole world stung.

'I'm not a whore!' she cried bitterly, jerking her chin away from him. This time she held his eyes and defied the mockery in them. 'And I wasn't then,

Mr Blakemore, so don't suggest such a thing again,' she finished huskily.

He was unimpressed by her vehemence and merely smiled down at her lithe body, scanning his mocking eyes over her creamy olive skin, the body he had once possessed so thoroughly.

Zoe felt his eyes like hot blades of steel on her bare flesh. It was as if she weren't wearing the cool crêpe evening dress, as if she were as naked as she'd been the night she'd spent with this man. The very thought of it raged through her flesh feverishly till the white crêpe was no longer cool but more a suffocating blanket.

'And it wasn't Mr Blakemore then,' he went on determinedly. 'You called me something more intimate, something in Greek, almost an incantation as I made love to you——'

'The night was a mistake!' Zoe cried wildly, her heart careering painfully. 'I made a terrible mistake——'

'No mistake, darling,' he grazed roughly, as if suddenly angry for some reason. Zoe held those cold eyes now, more in curiosity than in pleading despair. 'You were on loan to me that night in Switzerland,' he went on, devastatingly cuttingly, 'courtesy of Theodosius Koriakis, and how well you performed. You must be an asset to his empire, a real courtesan——'

Zoe turned and fled then, her beautiful face twisted with pain and her heart twisted by that desperate mistake she had made with Franc Blakemore. She had tried to forget, prayed he would never step into her life again, but he had and she couldn't bear it.

Kicking off her high heels, she ran barefoot through the gardens till she reached the warm sands of the beach, and then she slowed her pace, dragged her weary feet through the deep sand and let the tears fall. She slumped down by her special rock and huddled in the darkness and the past swept over her like molten-lava flow.

'I love you, Pierre,' Zoe whispered in the gardens of Theo's Swiss château, her hands clutching his tightly. She loved these business trips to Switzerland because of the secret meetings with her love. The château was always full of house guests and that's how she had come to meet Pierre. He worked for the Swiss bankers Theo employed to direct his millions and always stayed at the château when Theo and his entourage were in residence.

'But we must beware, *chérie*; Theo would be angry——'

'To hell with Theo!' Zoe laughed and tried to drag Pierre out of the shadows into the floodlit garden, to show the world their love. But Pierre held her back, in the shadows of the pines, way out of sight of the world.

'Come to my room later tonight, after the cocktail party.' Zoe giggled as she linked her arms around his neck.

He laughed. 'So naughty, *chérie*. I can't believe you want me to make love to you under your mentor's roof.'

'Forget Theo!' Zoe insisted with a laugh. 'If you love someone you want to make love to them, *n'est-ce pas?*'

Pierre shook his head in mock sufferance. 'I think it is not love, I think you want to get back at Theo for being so strict with you. He acts more like a possessive lover than your employer.'

'No!' Zoe cried insistently, angry now. Childishly she snatched her hands from his. 'Theo has no claims on me. I'm a free spirit. I work for him but I don't live for him. I can do as I please.'

But as she spoke the words she knew them not to be true. Theo had power over her and her mother. Once she had believed Theo to be her father but her mother had angrily rebuffed the query and refused to speak of it again. Zoe had gone to Theo himself to find out the truth about her parentage and he had been painfully honest. Theo and her mother, Heraklea, had grown up together in the Pelopennese. Later, Heraklea had gone to England to study, Theo to America. Heraklea fell in love with an Englishman and had an affair with him. Later he had refused to acknowledge that the child she was carrying was his. Theo had brought her back to the Greek islands and vowed to look after her and the coming child. Heraklea had never got over the pain of her rejection and even now still believed the man she loved would come after her. It was an obsession that had deprived Zoe of any maternal love. While the beautiful Heraklea waited for her lost lover she was happy for Theo to take over the raising of her child. Never a love-child, because Zoe had not brought her happiness: Zoe had been the cause of her lover's rejecting her.

So Zoe was illegitimate and carried the surname of a father she never knew, her mother believing that if one of them carried his name it would bring him back.

Theo kept her mother in genteel splendour in a small town not far from his own Greek splendour on a paradise island south-east of the Peloponnese. Her mother rarely ventured off the island, whereas Zoe travelled everywhere with Theo. He educated her in England and later insisted she join his business empire. She worked with a team of others organising his worldwide social and business calendar but though she worked with the team she was never one of them. She was different. She lived in Theo's houses. She was under Theo's thumb. She was often thought of as his mistress, sometimes his daughter, and often resented it, but was powerless to do anything about it. Theo owned her and her mother.

'If you can do as you please,' laughed Pierre, 'you can come to *my* room tonight, *chérie*,' he suggested in a conciliatory tone.

Zoe's dark eyes sparkled daringly. 'I just might, *chérie*,' she teased, and then, 'No, not might, I will!' she added decisively.

'But——'

'No buts, I will come to you,' she laughed, and after kissing him full on the lips turned and raced back to the hotel for a meeting with Theo and the team, then after the cocktail party that was to follow she would be free to go to Pierre.

People, people, people. Theo, who generated power and wealth, was always surrounded by a massive entourage of people. There was someone new this trip. A man called Blakemore. Theo had summoned him from America to tighten his own

personal security. Franc Blakemore was the highest
paid security adviser in the world, his work often
dangerous, always highly confidential. He worked
for ambassadors, royalty and the rich who could
afford him. There had been a buzz of interest
among the others at his arrival. Blakemore was
tough, Blakemore was legend and Blakemore was
gorgeous, twittered the female staff.

Zoe reluctantly agreed he was, but not half as
interesting as her delightful Pierre. She barely gave
the legend a glance at the party; she was lost in her
own fantasy world where Pierre was loving her and
asking her to marry him and she would accept and
then she would be free, really free.

Later she slipped away to Pierre's room but he
wasn't there—but he would come because he loved
her, she told herself dreamily. She waited by his
window in the unlit bedroom, gripping her hands
in anticipation and gazing down to the illuminated
gardens below, and then her heart stilled and her
pulses faded away and her fists tightened fearfully.
It wasn't possible...it couldn't be... That couldn't
be her beloved Pierre with another woman? They
were strolling leisurely through the gardens and
Pierre wasn't afraid to expose *her* to the world.
They stopped and kissed and were so obviously in
love that Zoe's heart tore agonisingly. Zoe knew
the girl and it made her pain worse. She was one
of the Swiss housekeeping force, a sweet girl—but
a maid, a mere maid.

Zoe clutched herself fiercely, the betrayal biting
into her flesh. Love was so dulling to the mind. She
should have picked up on Pierre's reluctance but
she hadn't. Even the suggestion to come to his room

was a bluff she had stupidly called. But of course he knew he wouldn't be here because he had somewhere else to go tonight!

A sob caught in her throat. Pierre didn't want her, had never wanted her, and no man ever would for fear of crossing Theo. She gouged her lower lip with self-pity and fought back the tears of rejection, but perhaps it was more than that... The girl was pretty; she, Zoe, had been told she was beautiful... but beauty could frighten off a man... and perhaps she just wasn't nice enough... Oh, God, what did the reasons matter? No one wanted her... no one would ever want her... even her father hadn't wanted her...

She spun as light suddenly slanted in from the opening door, bathing her in a shaft of golden brightness. That same golden light silhouetted a man in the doorway and she knew instantly who he was.

There was shock and fear at first, crackling down her spine and rushing her pulses once again, and then it was gone and curiosity took its place because he didn't speak. He had seen her, she was in no doubt of that, and recognised her too but why was he here in Pierre's room? She didn't know and couldn't ask and somehow it didn't matter.

Slowly he closed the door after him and there was a long pause as if he was accustoming his eyes to the darkness. Her eyes were already attuned to the moonlight in the room and she could see him well enough.

Slowly he came towards her and stopped inches from her. She could smell him, a warm, heady, musky smell. She could hear his deep, even

breathing in the stillness of the room and something so strange and disturbing pulsed deep inside
her that she felt faint with the power of it.

She didn't move, though. She should have spoken
but she didn't do that either. She simply stood where
she was and waited, her soft breath catching in her
throat.

He touched her, tentatively at first, almost afraid
she would vaporise away from him like a terrified
ghost. His hand smoothed down her cheek, now a
strong hand, a determined hand. It grazed down
her throat, lower and lower to the soft black silk
that brushed across her breasts.

His touch fanned and flamed her nerve-endings
and the air grew hot and heavy around her. She
knew then, in that strange, sensuous moment, that
she was committed to whatever this man had in
mind.

'You are so beautiful,' he breathed hoarsely, 'and
I want you very much.'

Zoe fluttered her eyes shut, her thick jet lashes
still glistening with unshed tears of rejection. But
this wasn't rejection. *He* wanted her, this man
wanted her and this man wasn't afraid to take what
he wanted. His mouth closed softly over hers, warm
and sensual, moving gently at first and then more
passionately when she parted her lips willingly
under his.

She wanted this stranger too, in every way. He
eased the pain of Pierre's betrayal with his mouth
and kisses, he reassured her that she was a desirable
woman, and as his arms encircled her and drew her
hard against his desire her head emptied of all sen-

sible reasoning, whipped away by a need to be loved, completely and without inhibition.

He slid the narrow silk straps of her dress from her shoulders, smouldered kisses over her breasts, suckled her inflamed nipples till she moaned out for a greater release. Frantically she splayed her fingers through his thick, dark hair, drawing him into her, demanding more and more.

'Steady, sweet one,' he soothed. 'The night is going to be a long one.'

Zoe laughed then, softly, temptingly, uncharacteristically. It was born out of a sudden nervous wave of doubt at what she was doing and was swept away on a shaft of need that knifed through her. She was desperate for freedom, the freedom to love and be loved and at whatever cost.

He slid her dress down over her hips and it slipped to the floor with a soft murmur. She touched him then, reached out and smoothed her fingers under his evening jacket, across a chest that was frighteningly taut and powerful. She mouthed kisses across his chin as she fumbled inexpertly with the buttons of his silk evening shirt. She didn't want to appear naïve, and she tried to make every movement assertive as if she knew what she was doing.

Dear God, if he knew ... But he wouldn't ... she wouldn't let him know.

His breath was so irregular now that it seemed to fill the room. His kisses were more ardent and Zoe rose to the clamour and insistence of her own need. The dispensing of the rest of their clothes was done expertly by this man, hastily but with quiet assurance. He knew what he was doing and Zoe was happy with that. She needed guidance from this man and she needed love from him.

The joy of touching his naked flesh, of reaching out and smoothing her near-trembling hands over his powerful body surpassed anything she had ever experienced before in her life. He was beautiful, magnificent, taut-skinned with strong yet yielding body hair. She pressed her warm lips to his chest and felt the need to please him as well as demanding pleasure for herself.

'You certainly know what you're doing,' he murmured as he stilled her inquisitive hands. Then he lifted her and lowered her to the bed.

He was wrong—she didn't know what she was doing; it was all instinctive, and yet every exploration pleased him and she swelled with pride and grew braver with each caress. Her mind was empty of all but the need to love this man and be loved in return. And he *was* loving her, so beautifully, as if she was so very special to him. Her thoughts went no further than the delicious exchanged kisses and caresses and as his touch became more intimate she wanted to cry with the sweet pleasure of it all.

'Do you like that, beautiful one?' he asked throatily as he stroked her inner thighs, moving closer to the part of her that ached for his touch.

Zoe couldn't speak because of the emotion and need that seemed to swell her throat, and she simply nodded her dark head against his shoulder. Please don't let him know, she prayed. His touch reached its target, so sensuously that she had to bite back the cry that came to her lips, a cry like some wild animal of the forest. He stroked her so tenderly that she blossomed under the touch, pressed herself into him and clutched at his hair.

Suddenly he was towering over her, predatory and powerful, parting her thighs with his legs. She closed her eyes tightly in expectation of the pain, her fingers coiled into his back in sharpened defence, but there was no pain, only hard, fearful, desperate pressure that brought a moan of deep desire from them both.

'Perfect,' he grated raggedly, 'you're just perfect.' He moved more urgently, more assertively, and Zoe was spun out of reality and into a fiery world of frantic movement that drove her to the brink of an ecstasy she had never known existed. His kisses were hot and hard as he drove into her and she clung to him and cried out for the first time, declaring her love in her native tongue, repeating it over and over again.

She climaxed before him, a desperate explosion that shocked her with its overwhelming feeling of heat and release, and then the tempest within her rose again as he moved more urgently within her, swelling and expanding and driving her into a fantasy world of tumbling liquid emotion. And then he cried out his intention and she closed her intimacy around him, drawing him down with her into that vortex of heat and fire where they were the only two people in the world, floating in its mysterious vapours.

It should have been the end but he was an insatiable lover and the night went on and on as he had predicted. More discoveries, more sweet pleasures, deeper and deeper into a world of love and desire they sank. They kissed and touched and left no mystery undiscovered. It was a lifetime of loving gathered into a few frantic hours, as if the world wouldn't rise with the dawn.

And the dawn, when it came, was harsh and cruel and punishing in the reality it brought to Zoe. She awoke, languid and soft with his arms coiled protectively around her, and then life seeped back into her liquid bones and all her fears and doubts were realised as she turned her face to the stranger she loved.

And she did love him, this legend, Franc Blakemore, who was sleeping so soundly beside her. She didn't know him, probably never would, but she knew she loved him. If she had a girlfriend to confide in she would undoubtedly say that you always loved the first man you went with or, worse, that it was just passion and a treacherous deluder of the heart. But Zoe knew differently. She had Greek blood in her veins, and Greek girls only gave themselves to their true love, so she must love this man to have done what she had. Yet she hadn't loved him before he had made love to her; she had been in love with Pierre... She bit her lip in confusion. She was twenty and should understand these things, but she didn't. No one had taught her about love, no one had ever been close enough to her to teach her anything about life beyond Theodosius Koriakis's protective nucleus.

She slid out of the bed, dressed silently and then turned to look down on the Blakemore man, who slept on. It would be easy to avoid him for the rest of their time in Switzerland. Theo's trips were always frantic. She wouldn't be involved in the talks about Theo's security arrangements; that was other people's jobs. No, she would never see him again.

Sadly she tiptoed from the room and as she closed the door behind her she understood what the night had been all about. The housekeeper allocated the guest-rooms. On the last trip Pierre had been in this room; this time Franc Blakemore's name was in the slot on the carved oak door. In her foolish eagerness she hadn't looked, in her foolish eagerness she had waited and given her love to a stranger, and he had accepted it willingly. Her heart lay as cold as a stone in her breast at how he might interpret their night of love. But they would never meet again, so what did it matter? But somehow it did, achingly so.

In spite of the heat of the night Zoe shivered and dug her heels into the sand and clutched her knees to her chin. Moisture misted her brow and the white crêpe dress clung damply to her back. She wiped the moisture from her forehead with the back of her hand and let out a small sob. So now she knew how he had in fact interpreted that night. He had thought she was on loan, some sexual favour from Theo, an added bonus for his services. Oh, why had he come to Theo's party tonight? Why had he come back into her life when it was the last thing she wanted?

'Zoe?'

The call came softly in the dark night and Zoe shrank back against the rock.

He hauled her to her feet, pulled her away from her refuge and into silvery moonlight. 'You forget I can see in the dark,' he husked softly.

'Like a damned panther!' she spat. 'Let me go! You forget who I am!' she cried in defence, hoping the veiled threat would make him let her go.

He laughed at her paltry attempt to cow him. 'Theo's mistress, some say, Theo's illegitimate daughter, say others. I wonder how you explain yourself to your lovers?'

'I have no lovers—not like you, who has a mistress in every embassy in the world, *they say*!'

She hadn't known that when she had allowed him to love her. That painful revelation had come from one of the other secretaries, the very morning after her night of love with the man. No wonder he had been such a willing lover, no wonder he hadn't asked questions. He was used to women giving themselves to him so unconditionally.

She tried to wriggle her arm from his grasp but he held on, though keeping her at a distance as if he feared injury from her, or perhaps it was with disdain. Yes, women gave themselves to him and he took them, and she had been as weak as the next, and men had no respect for women like that.

Shame hit her then and her whole body seemed to crumble. He reached out and caught and drew her against him, then took a sharp intake of breath before lowering his mouth to hers.

The kiss took her by surprise and for a second there was blank astonishment and then a fearful rush of emotions as she realised nothing had changed in those past three years, though she had fought it furiously. He had haunted her very existence, been with her every painful hour of the day and loved her all the way through the agonising nights. And now he was here, in the flesh, and be-

lieving her love had been on loan for that erotic
night in Switzerland.

'Why are you here?' she sobbed as she wrenched
her burning mouth away from his.

He held her by the shoulders and smoothed his
thumbs tantalisingly over her damp skin.

'It doesn't matter why I'm here; what matters is,
are the conditions the same as last time?'

Shocked, she broke into Greek, spurning the
suggestion with every invective she could muster,
insulting him and denying she was ever what he accused her of. In the moonlight she saw his face
harden and his grip on her tightened viciously.

'Stop that! You're no wretched peasant so don't
smart-mouth me in a foreign language again!'

'You bastard, you bastard!' she raged. 'Is that
better? Do you understand *that*?'

'Fully,' he grated, not releasing her from his
clutches. 'So now we have one thing clear between
us: you're not a whore, though you scream like
one.'

'And I suppose I'm supposed to be grateful for
that benevolent statement, am I?' she retorted sarcastically, refusing to fully acknowledge the absol-
ution he had offered. 'Why are you here?' she
repeated when he made no reply.

'Why would you like me to be here?'

'I have no thoughts in that direction,' she replied
tightly. He couldn't possibly know how deeply he
had affected her life since Switzerland; nor would
he ever.

'I can't believe that. Tonight you ran like a terrified fawn and I'd like to know why. You owe me
that at least.'

'I ran because I was threatened,' she retorted hotly. 'By you. You made no attempt to hide your disdain for me when Theo introduced us just now——'

'Because I read the drop-dead look in your eyes as soon as you saw me. In my business attack is the best defence.'

'I'm not your *business*, Mr Blakemore. I was the whore on loan that night and nothing else. We owe each other nothing.'

She could just make out the sneer on his mouth. 'So now you are willingly admitting to what I accused you of. What a crazy, mixed-up child you are.'

'I'm no child!'

'You act like one—out of bed, not in it. Between the sheets you are something else, lovely one.'

'Shut up!' Zoe cried squeakily. 'Just you shut up and leave me alone!' She tried to run but he still held her tightly and she jerked back into his arms, so close that she was aware of his warm breath, his smell, his strength. She had known it all once before and loved it all. And the passing of time—had it changed anything? Shocked, she shrank in his hold. If he pulled her down into the warm sand now, would she give herself as willingly as before—just as all the others did?

'Why do you tremble against me, sweet one? Does the past trouble you or do the same passions clamour for release as they did so erotically once before?'

'I... I don't——' she husked awkwardly. Her breath hurt in her throat and she was desperate for escape, but this man wasn't going to allow it. What did he want of her?

'You don't know?' he mocked and then laughed softly in the hot night air. 'Well, darling, you'll have long enough to make a decision about that.'

'A-about what?'

'Whether or not the business arrangement will stretch to include you in my bed as before.'

'Just what are you saying?' she breathed heavily. 'What business arrangement? What the devil are you talking about?'

His grip lessened and one hand slid down her arm and grasped her hand. 'I think we'd better get back to the party. Tomorrow Theo will explain the arrangement.' He tried to lead her back along the beach but Zoe held back, pulled back and snatched her hand from his. The moon lit his face and she could see him clearly now, see the unexpected frown on his brow.

'No!' she cried. She stood and defied him. 'I'm not going anywhere with you. I want you to explain to me what you mean. What business arrangement and what do you mean, I'll have long enough to make a decision . . . about . . . about——?'

'Loving me again,' he reminded her and then laughed again cynically. 'But of course it wasn't love, was it? It was your job, nothing more, nothing less.'

He gave her space to answer that but she didn't fill it. She could have saved her honour and pleaded that she had adored him that night, but you couldn't admit to such crazy reasoning with him. No one could love a stranger unless he or she were mad. She obviously was.

'I don't understand you,' she breathed innocently, shaking her head till her jet hair whispered around her face in the breeze. 'I don't understand you and what you want of me, and I want to know now, not tomorrow and not with...not with Theo,' she finished lamely. She lowered her head and he was quick to raise her chin with his fingers.

'Are you afraid of him?'

Her dark brown eyes blinked open widely at the sudden concern in his voice and then they narrowed defensively. 'Of course not! He's not my lover as you undoubtedly think, nor my...nor my keeper.' She faltered over that because lately it seemed as if he was. He'd always been protective with her, more so of late when that paternal care had turned to a suffocating obsession, as if he was terrified to let her out of his sight. If Theo knew what this man believed about her on that Swiss night—that she had been on loan with his compliments...if he knew that they had made love so passionately under his roof... She shuddered to think. Theo would kill for that insult to his Greek honour—he'd kill her for giving herself so wantonly and this Blakemore for taking her.

'And yet you jump at his every command——'

'I do not!' Her bare feet twisted in the sand. 'I...I owe him for my upbringing, his love and protection——'

'And you repay that debt by giving your body to his business acquaintances?' Franc uttered scornfully.

She didn't react to that, not physically by striking a blow at him, but mentally she scarred him for the suggestion. He didn't know that she had been in his room by mistake and if she told him, how could she explain why she had allowed him to love her? Because she had been so lonely and needed someone. A man like him wouldn't understand such things.

'Come,' he said softly, not pressing her for an answer, 'we must get back to the party before we're missed.'

'You're no different from the rest of them,' Zoe muttered as she reluctantly dropped into step beside him.

'Clarify that.'

Bravely she went on. 'Everyone is afraid of Theo, everyone except me.'

Franc Blakemore laughed. 'I fear no man, sweet Zoe; remember that in the future, and I'm glad to hear you don't fear him either.'

'Why should you be glad to hear that? I'm nothing to you, and why should I have to re-member how bloody fearless you are in the future? You aren't in *my* future.'

'But I am, and in *our* future you will desist from swearing. I don't like it and I won't tolerate it.'

Zoe splayed her fingers and made a very in-sulting Greek gesture, and Franc snapped at her wrist so swiftly that she had no time to pull away.

'And don't do that either. It doesn't become you. When you live with me I want none of this rebel-lious Greek peasant melodrama. You're not the only kid in the world who doesn't know who her father is——'

'How dare you? How bloody dare you——?'

His mouth clamped over hers, forcing her lips apart, drawing the very breath from her lungs. The kiss was long and impassioned but stinging with a punishing power. When he drew back from her at last she saw the gleam of iron anger in his dark eyes.

'Swear at me again and I'll do that again. Again and again until you learn.'

Zoe bit her lip and stared up at him, too stunned to answer. She could so easily push this man to the extremes of his patience but the consequences would be too painful. He saw his own mouth as a punishment; she saw it that way too, but for very different reasons.

Her head spun crazily. She parted her lips and whispered throatily in the hot, dry night air.

'What do you mean? How do you know I don't know who my father is? What did you mean when...when you said when I live with you?'

His anger was abated now but there was still grim determination in his eyes. His lips drew into a line faintly resembling a smile, though in the next few seconds she could see nothing to smile about.

'You're on loan again, sweet one. Theodosius Koriakis has kindly offered me your services for a period as long as it takes. You will work for me, live with me, do precisely what I tell you to do.' He reached out and grazed the remnants of his kiss from her lips with his thumb. 'And what delights we have ahead of us, what nights and delights. I've waited three long years to sample your boss's hospitality once again and now he's handing you to me on a plate.'

Zoe's mouth gaped open; she was shattered, demoralised and stunned. She couldn't take this in.

It was all too much. Theo was crazy, so was she, and so was this man standing in front of her.

'So, Zoe, what have you got to say to that?'

She jutted her chin forward and, emulating her mother's fiery temper, she opened her mouth and let forth every Greek insult she knew and then breathlessly added, 'And if your Greek isn't advanced enough to translate that I'll do it for you, censored of course: go take a jump at yourself, Franc Blakemore, because you...you are...*pathetic*!'

She turned and strode back to the villa across the sands, pretty sure he wouldn't come after her. When you insulted a Greek man's sexual prowess you didn't live to repeat it, and when you gave the same insult to a jumped-up Anglo-American by the name of Franc Blakemore the truth would hit home, but your skin was safe. He had understood, she knew that for sure, but he wouldn't do anything about it because she lived under Theodosius Koriakis's protection and no one crossed Theo, not even *bloody* Franc Blakemore.

A shiver ran through her as she heard him laugh behind her. It rose in momentum to a roar and with a sob she clamped her hands over her ears and broke into a run, faster and faster till she hoped she would die with the effort.

CHAPTER TWO

'I WON'T go, Theo, I absolutely won't go!'

'You do as you are told, Zoe, dear,' Theo told her calmly the next morning, none the worse for last night's birthday celebrations.

Zoe was hungover but not through drink. She had spent a sleepless night with Franc Blakemore's laughter ringing in her ears like a death-knell. Now this morning she was facing Theo in his study, and he wasn't listening; he just wasn't.

'I don't want to work for him, and why me? Why not one of the other secretaries? Any one of them is capable of re-organising his agency for him.'

'He specifically asked for you.' Theo sat down at his desk and pressed the intercom. 'Send Mr Blakemore in.'

Zoe's heart went to pulp. So Franc Blakemore had specifically asked for her; that hadn't been his story. He had said Theo had offered him her services. One or both of them was lying. Wasn't there a man in this world who didn't draw the long bow?

She stood by the open patio doors and gazed blindly out down to the beach. Days ago she had been yearning for her freedom, yearning to be away from Theo's claustrophobic protection. Greek fathers were possessive and though he wasn't her real father he acted so. She was twenty-three and travelled the world widely with him, but she was never free, really free. And this last year had been the worst. He had suffocated her, but now he was offering some sort of freedom—but with the last person on earth she wanted to be with.

'I don't want to say this in front of him,' Zoe breathed hotly, swivelling to face the Greek millionaire behind his desk, rushing her words before Blakemore came in, 'but I don't like him, Theo—I don't like him, I don't trust him. You...you know what I mean.' She lowered her dark eyes, fluttered her eyelashes nervously, hoping her surrogate father would get the message.

Theo laughed, a deep, gravelly laugh that bounced off the cool marble floor and seemed to slap Zoe in the face.

'The man is the only person in the world I truly trust, otherwise I wouldn't agree to his suggestion,' he chuckled. 'Don't worry, Zoe, dear, your honour is safe with him.'

Dear God, if he knew... 'But Theo, they say he has a mistress in every embassy,' she protested wildly. 'The girls say...'

Theo laughed. 'I'm sure the girls wish they were those mistresses. What have I told you about listening to gossip?'

'It isn't gossip!' Zoe insisted. 'You only have to look at him to know.'

Theo's beady eyes glistened but there was no humour there now. 'He's good-looking, yes, as good-looking as I was at his age, but there was only one woman for me and she eluded me. I looked no further. Blakemore looks no further either.'

'What do you mean, he looks no further?' Zoe whispered. She had never heard Theo talk that way before. The lover who had eluded him must surely be her mother, but Franc Blakemore—why did he look no further? Somehow that was far more important than her mother and Theo's problems.

'You can ask him some time; you'll be spending enough time with each other.' His eyes held hers suddenly. 'You have nothing to fear from him, Zoe,' he said almost softly. 'Like all red-blooded men he takes what he needs, but he would never take advantage of you. Not even Franc Blakemore would be foolish enough to dishonour my trust, I promise you that.'

It wasn't Theo's promise she needed! Zoe thought dismally, and, besides, he already had taken advantage, had already dishonoured that trust, absolutely and thoroughly.

She tensed as Franc Blakemore strode into the study looking cool in white trousers and a white shirt so superbly cut that they looked more expensive than Theo's. It suddenly occurred to her that this was the first time she had seen him properly in daylight. Her colour heightened at that shameful thought.

He smiled at her, a very open smile, white and beautifully executed as if he had nothing in the world to hide from a soul. She could blurt it out now, the truth—that this man had already made love to her; but the horror of it all was that she couldn't live with the aftermath of her revelations: the horror of Theo knowing what sort of a woman he had raised, the horror of what he would do to Blakemore.

She didn't smile back at him but went and stood by Theo, placing her hand on his shoulder, for once in her life desperately wanting his protection.

'You can go now, Zoe,' Theo told her, patting her hand in what he thought was a reassuring gesture. 'Pack your things and be ready to leave in an hour.'

'No, Theo,' she cried, noting the tensing of Theo's shoulder muscles beneath her fingers. She had crossed him before and suffered at the hands of his temper—not physically, but his words always hurt her so deeply with their threat to disown her mother, who had no other support but Theo's. But her sanity was on the line here.

'I don't want to leave you and Mother,' she tried, anxiously glancing at Franc in the thin hope he might relent and not insist on this ridiculous arrangement. 'Mother wouldn't want me to leave.' She knew she sounded childish and petulant but at this moment she felt so very vulnerable.

'Your mother is in complete agreement over this, Zoe,' Theo told her coolly. 'Now do as you are told and get ready.'

Her hand dropped to her side. It was hopeless to argue and that angered her more than the thought that her mother was agreeing to this. Heraklea never stood up to him, but perhaps she knew it was useless, whereas Zoe couldn't accept that yet and went at Theo like a dumb goat butting a brick wall.

'Am I permitted to ask where I'm going?' she said haughtily.

'No, you are not,' grated Theo, and stood up to hand Blakemore a fax. 'But it will be warm, so pack accordingly.'

'I'm going to hell, am I?' she cried as she wrenched open the study door. 'Well, anywhere would be *heaven* rather than here where I'm not wanted!'

She slammed the door on them both, just catching a moan of exasperation from Theo and a knowing, sympathetic look directed at Theo from Blakemore.

Zoe didn't know whom she despised most at that moment.

'How dare you come in here without knocking?' Zoe protested half an hour later. She sat cross-legged on her bed, flicking through a magazine, seeing nothing but the supercilious face of Franc Blakemore leering up at her from the glossy pages. Now he was here, in her bedroom, uninvited. That boded well for her future.

'Why haven't you packed?' he asked. He came across the room and snatched the magazine from her and tossed it on to the bedside chair.

Zoe leaned over and snatched it back. 'Do you mind?'

'I do, very much.' He glanced at his watch. 'We have a boat to catch, a flight to pick up on in Athens, so stop sulking and get ready.'

She stretched lazily. 'I don't think I'll be going.'

'You will; now stop being a silly girl——'

'I'm not a silly girl and don't speak to me as if I were five years old!' Zoe hissed.

'Of course, I was forgetting—you're a very sexy, erotic, demanding young courtesan who does a very nice line in alternative pouting. No, you are not five years old but you act it, and I'll go along with that—but remember that naughty, disobedient children occasionally get their backsides tanned.

Now unless you want me to bring tears to your eyes I suggest you get off that bed and pack.'

Zoe moved like a turbo-powered jelly. Her hands trembled as she snatched a bundleful of springy silk underwear from her chest of drawers and flung them on the bed.

Franc Blakemore leaned against the dressing-room door and grinned widely. 'I'm sure Freud would make a meal of that.'

'What?' Zoe blazed, her 'backside' still stinging from the verbal lashing he had bestowed on her.

'The first thing you are preparing to pack is your underwear. I wonder what you are anticipating?'

'Not what you're thinking.' She went for her toiletries then. 'Women always pack their underwear first.'

'Afraid of being caught with their knickers down?'

'No, afraid of being run over by a bus; now get out of my way—I want to get the rest of my clothes.'

He didn't move. 'I think you have enough already,' he mocked. 'In fact too much. Where we are going there isn't much call for passion-peach undies and French perfume.'

'Where are we going, then?' Zoe snapped her fingers and drawled sarcastically, 'Oh, I forgot, to hell and back; well, I haven't been before so perhaps you'll enlighten me as to what exactly I do need— an asbestos body-stocking?'

'Could be a trifle debilitating—to us both,' he added with another infuriating grin. 'Why don't you just come in that delightfully scented skin of yours? It served you well enough three years ago.'

'Three years ago I was two years old; now I'm five and a hundred years older,' she snorted.

'That sounded very cynical.'

'You got the point, then?'

'Between the eyes where it was aimed for,' Franc replied.

'Good. Now will you shift out of the way while I pack the rest of my things?'

He eased himself away from the door and opened it for her. 'Enough for... say a bag this big.' He held his hands about a foot apart.

'Don't be silly.' She hauled a shift from the wardrobe. 'I couldn't possibly get all my clothes in a bag that size even if I had one, which I don't!'

'But I have.' Franc Blakemore drew a polythene bag from his trouser pocket. 'I'd very much appreciate it if you could fill this——'

Zoe snatched it from him and blew into it. 'With hot air.' She knotted it and pushed it back into his hand. 'Though you have enough of your own.'

'I'm serious, lovely one,' he grated with just a hint of a smirk to his mouth. 'We are travelling light, and I mean light.' He punctured the bag and squeezed the air from it before handing it back to her.

Zoe snatched it and glowered at him. 'Are you serious?' She'd had enough of this game. He really was being very silly.

'Absolutely. You'll find everything you need when we get there, but for travelling I want you to keep everything to the minimum. A toothbrush would be pushing it a bit.'

'You *are* serious!' Zoe cried incredulously then her mouth tightened defiantly and she folded her arms across her chest. 'I'm not going anywhere with you till you tell me where we are going and for how long and what exactly this is all about. I can't believe you couldn't hire any number of willing secretaries to work for you. Why me?'

'Because you are the only one I want,' he volunteered, his voice heavy with meaning.

Zoe felt hot all over. She'd fantasised often enough that he would come back into her life and utter those words, but to mean them, in a loving, caring way, not like this, dripping with crude suggestion.

'Because you think you can take my body on demand along with my secretarial skills?' she bravely blurted.

'I dare say if push came to shove I could take many a secretary on demand, but I doubt I would enjoy them as much as I enjoyed you. You really are the very best, you know, and I don't mean at shorthand.'

She pushed her way past him and he followed her. She stood by the patio doors that opened on to her private balcony and refused to face him. 'Is that supposed to be a compliment?'

'Yes,' he replied smoothly.

She turned then and he was so close behind her that she nearly bumped into him. 'I don't accept it as one,' she said quietly.

'Well, you should, because that was the way it was meant.' His hand reached up and touched her cheek and she flinched away from him. He frowned. 'Why did you do that?'

'Because . . . because I don't want you touching me.'

'You didn't object before——'

'Before when? Before my life ended?' She spun away from him, back into the room, to put distance between them. 'Look, this is all crazy. I don't want to work for you, in any capacity. I'm not the courtesan you think I am and I'm not going to bed with you again, ever!'

'And why not?'

'And why not?' she echoed almost hysterically. 'Because I don't want to—can't you get that into that arrogant head of yours? I don't like you, in or out of bed. You understood what I said to you in Greek last night and you just laughed. Well, it was no joke, Mr High Security. I meant it; you did nothing for me—zilch!'

She couldn't even anger him. She stared in disbelief as he leaned nonchalantly back on the white stone walls and actually smiled again.

'You lie delightfully, sweet Zoe. Anyone can be good but not many achieve perfection—but we did that night, both of us.'

'Don't fool yourself,' she seethed.

'I don't. I know exactly what I am good at,' he told her.

'Most things, no doubt!'

'I wouldn't be so presumptuous. I'm a rotten polo player.'

Her eyes narrowed. 'This is all one big game to you, isn't it? Ride my emotions as hard as you can and then strike where it counts. I'd say you were an expert polo player.'

'And you're very good at riding your high horse. Unsaddle yourself, Zoe, and come down to earth

and tell me why you feel so bad about that night
we spent together.'

'I don't feel bad about it!' she retorted hotly.

'You die a thousand deaths when I accuse
you——'

'Of being a whore!' she finished for him.

'Courtesan,' he corrected drily. 'I much prefer
that description—a courtesan in the court of
Theodosius Koriakis.'

'It all means the same thing,' Zoe told him
breathlessly. 'You think I was on loan from Theo
that night. You take great delight in ramming it at
me at every opportunity. Why do you do that when
you know it isn't true? You must know that Theo
wouldn't make such an arrangement. He isn't
perfect but he has honour and morals and in-
tegrity——'

'Which his beautiful charge hasn't.'

Zoe coloured, with rage and shame. 'I have!' She
then realised he was pushing her. Her eyes misted.
'Why are you doing this?' she breathed softly,
pleadingly. 'You're pushing me for some sort of
explanation.' She shrugged hopelessly. 'I can't give
you one.'

'You can't tell me why you were waiting for me
in my room, why you wanted me to make love to
you?' he questioned, as if he really cared what her
answer would be.

She shook her head and lowered her eyes.

'Come now, Zoe. You claim Theo didn't loan
you out for the night——' He held his hand up to
still the protest that was already forming on her
lips. 'OK, let's forget that. Theo didn't loan you
out. You were there of your own free will, waiting

for me.' He drew a deep breath and was about to add something more but Zoe beat him to it.

'And you made love to me—made love to me just like that. You seduced me without even asking——'

Her fury rose as he started to laugh softly. 'You really are quite incredible, Zoe. Gifts like you I don't turn away. You were there for the taking——'

'Stop it! Just you stop it!' She went to rush for the door but he was quicker. He caught her and scooped at her wrist and raised the back of her hand to his lips.

'And just you stop that too!' she hissed painfully.

He held her hand, smoothing his kiss from her soft skin with his thumb. 'Listen, sweet one, I'm not fighting you. We're going to have to live and work together for a while, and fighting is out if we are to make a go of it; lying is out, too. I want to know the truth, Zoe. I want to know——'

'Why I was a pushover?'

'I wouldn't put it like that.'

'No, you prefer crudity, don't you? Calling me awful names.'

'I'm sorry if I offended you. Maybe I was trying to clear my own conscience. I don't sleep with whores.'

Zoe allowed a cynical smile to irritate him. 'You didn't know that I wasn't that night,' she suggested acidly, 'so that puts paid to your holier-than-thou virtues.'

'I repeat, I don't sleep with whores,' he told her coldly, tightening his grip on her hand.

Zoe opened her deep brown eyes widely. 'But you slept with *me*,' she husked sarcastically, realising she had him in a spot and was going to enjoy it to the full. 'You didn't know that I *wasn't* on loan from Theo. You took what you thought was on offer, and though no money changed hands it was the same thing, you know.' She smiled sweetly. 'You, Franc Blakemore, and all men like you, are victims of your own weaknesses. You wanted, you took, end of story. Don't try and probe my motivations to mist over the truth of your own. It takes two to fulfil a transaction, seller and buyer.'

'I started out wanting a simple answer to a simple question. I didn't ask for a spare rib being thrown at me. What a complex lady you are.'

Zoe raised a dark brow. 'Yes, I'm a Gemini. Two sides to my face. One half of me is all Greek, the other very European. I have Greek morals and thoughts but the European part of me is very liberated.'

'And that was the part that made love to me in Switzerland, the liberated part?' There was mockery interlaced in his words.

She swallowed and wanted to be anywhere but here in her bedroom with this man. He twisted everything she said. She was liberated, in her mind, but not the way he thought. She took a breath. There was only one way to get out of this.

'You said you wanted a simple answer to a simple question—why did I let you make love to me. I'll give it to you, and let's hope that will be the end of it all——'

'Now we're getting somewhere,' he breathed and smiled mockingly at her. 'I wait with bated breath.'

Seething inwardly, Zoe bit back the impulse to scream, 'Wait on,' and storm away from him in a huff. It had to end, all his fearful accusations and suggestive innuendoes. Bravely she spoke out, words spoken especially slowly for impact, for her own benefit as well as his. Perhaps if she said them earnestly enough she would believe them herself. 'You were a mistake, Franc Blakemore. Unbelievable as it may sound, I got the wrong bedroom. I...I thought you were someone else. I was waiting for my lover, you see, not you. All the time you were making love to me I thought you were someone else...' Her voice trailed away to a whisper at the terrible lie she had spoken. She had known—oh, how she had known exactly what she had done and welcomed him into her secret self.

It was then he started to laugh, softly, shaking his arrogant dark head in disbelief. 'Sorry, sweetheart, I don't buy that. Till me you'd never had a lover——'

'Of course I had!' she blurted defensively. Oh, God, he'd known, and it was all getting worse than ever. 'I was having an...an affair with...with a Frenchman——'

'Don't, Zoe.' He said it softly, almost pleadingly. 'Don't try and make out you're something you're not.'

Her throat dried and she couldn't even swallow now. He took everything from her and crushed it underfoot. He knew everything and she knew nothing.

'You've never had a lover because you've never had the freedom to take one; that and the fact that no one ever dared approach you——'

'You did!' she bit back.

'Theo holds no fears for me, and you have slightly strayed off the point. I didn't approach you; you were there for the taking.' She didn't answer and he lifted her chin to look deeply into her dark eyes. 'Was that why you let me love you that night—because no man had ever dared before?'

'No!' she breathed desperately, and then jerked her chin away from his fingers. 'I mean yes, yes, that was it...'

She did push him then; her hands came up and firmly shoved him away from her. She went to her bed and started to fling her underwear back into her drawer. 'I'm not going with you, to work for you or to put up with all this aggravation.' She straightened up suddenly and faced him, her face flushed with vibrant determination. 'I made a mistake that night and I don't want to pay for it for the rest of my life. I refuse to go with you and if you insist I'll...I'll tell Theo what happened that night.'

Franc Blakemore came and stood the other other side of the bed. He looked cool and in command while she looked and felt very much out of control. 'If you did then you *would* pay for it the rest of your life. I know Theo well enough to know he would make you pay dearly for that——'

'And you too!' Zoe blazed indignantly. 'And that would be the point of the exercise—to see you pay for what you are putting me through.'

Franc eased his hands back into his trouser pockets and he smiled. 'Zoe, don't you ever learn? I wouldn't suffer; men rarely do——'

'A knife in your back in some dark alley when you least expect it would make you suffer!'

'Not Theo's style.'

'He'd ruin you——'

Franc shook his head. 'He knows my worth.' He let out a deep sigh. 'No, Zoe, only two people would suffer by your revelations; you and someone else.'

'Oh, yes? And who would that someone else be?'

'Your mother.'

Zoe's hand froze around the bottle of Obsession she was returning to her dressing-table. She slammed it down angrily. Always her mother. Was she to spend the rest of her days paying for her mother's mistake? She could just imagine what Theo would say if she admitted to her night of love with Franc Blakemore; like mother, like daughter. Was that why Theo was so obsessive about her, sick at the thought that she might make the same mistake? Her fingers tightened around the bottle of perfume. Obsession. Theo had bought it for her and now she knew the true meaning of his obsession with her. Many years ago her mother had hurt Theo. Perhaps they had been betrothed as youngsters before her mother had fallen for someone else. But she didn't feel sorry for Theo. He wasn't doing either of them any favours by looking after them so well; it was more a term of imprisonment for them both, a punishment. Her mother accepted her exile, but why should the daughter? She hadn't sinned. Except she had now.

She looked warily across at Franc and was surprised to see him watching her wrestling with her thoughts. His eyes penetrated deeply and she wondered if he read minds.

'You're just saying that to save your own skin,' she whispered.

'Put it to the test, then,' he answered quietly.

It wasn't fair, life wasn't fair. She loved her mother. She couldn't take that risk. Zoe bit her lip. 'OK, you win. I won't breathe a word; not for your skin—I don't care a damn for it—but for mine and my mother's. You're right, as I expect you are always right about everything. Women don't have a chance in this so-called liberated world of ours——'

'Spare me all that,' Franc cut in, glancing at his watch. 'I've yet to meet a female who doesn't have total——'

'Spare me all that praying mantis spiel too,' Zoe bit back. 'It bores me to death, talking of which I would rather be dead than work for you.'

Franc let out a wearisome sigh. 'Well, Zoe, my love, you're no good to me dead.'

'So I don't have to come with you?' she asked hopefully.

He smiled and shook his head. 'You do. It's all arranged, and think of it this way—I'm offering you your freedom.'

'Freedom?' she wailed and then lifted her chin. 'If I come with you will I have any freedom? Can I live where I like? Can I take a lover?'

He grinned widely and Zoe could have happily cut his throat for not taking her seriously. 'Two out of three "no"s to that,' he laughed.

'Oh, so at least I'm free to take a lover!' she spiked back.

'No, you are not free to take a lover—unless it's me, of course—and you are not free to live where

you like; you will live with me and, yes, you will
have your freedom. Freedom to walk under the stars
at night, freedom to swim and collect shells and
freedom to cook me a wonderful meal every night.'

Zoe protested hotly. 'Cook for you? I'm not
going to keep house for you——'

'You'll have to. Where we are going there is a
dire shortage of home help.'

'You're teasing me,' she spluttered, but knew he
wasn't. Oh, how she hated Theo for setting this up.
She frowned suddenly. And why had Theo set all
this up? Franc Blakemore comes back into his life
after an absence of three years and demands her
services and he agrees.

She opened her mouth to speak but Franc un-
plunged his hands from his pockets and came towards her. 'Sorry to have to rush you but we really
must go—and please don't argue, Zoe.' He took
her by the shoulders and held her firmly. 'Arguing
has cost you your underwear because now there
really isn't enough time to pack it——'

'But——'

'But no more arguing. We must go.'

Suddenly he was deeply serious. She read it in
the tightening muscles at his jawline, at the sudden
darkness of his eyes. She felt a prickle of fear and
then it was gone as he steered her towards the
bedroom door.

'I must say goodbye to Theo and my
mother——' she began.

'There isn't time. Your mother and Theo don't
expect any fond farewells.'

How true, and how strange Franc Blakemore had
insight to her life. She loved her mother because

she was her mother but they were oceans apart. Sometimes she loved Theo but he wasn't her real father. No, no one expected any fond farewells.

As Franc Blakemore hurried her down the curving marble stairway of the villa to the car parked outside Zoe had a range of mixed emotions coursing through her veins. She didn't want this job with Franc and yet she did. It was true—Franc was offering her a certain freedom; often enough of late she had wanted to be free of Theo and the entourage, to live a life of her choice. But in that way Franc Blakemore was offering nothing different. It sounded as if she was going to be bound to him as she'd been bound to Theo all her life. But a change of scene was something and she was going to hell—wherever that might be—with the man she loved.

She watched his face as he slammed the passenger door after her. She did still love him. She had often wondered if she came face to face with him again would that feeling still be there. She didn't even know him, but her love hadn't waned over the three years. But it was a painful love and not in the least ecstatic as it should be; that was because it wasn't returned. He had come back for a secretary, not a lover, though she felt sure he would expect her to fall into his bed once again.

She wouldn't, though; she knew that with a dragging certainty. She wouldn't be used again. Franc had said it all: she was on loan, for as long as it took. For as long as what took? she asked herself. As long as it took for him to grow tired of her?

Theo unexpectedly ran down the steps at the last minute and kissed her on the cheek; that was surprising enough, but then he did something that sent a chill of apprehension down Zoe's spine. He put his heavy arms around Franc Blakemore and hugged him before he got into the car, as one Greek to another, one good friend to another.

'You... you know Theo very well, don't you?' she breathed as they sped towards the marina on the other side of the island.

Franc drove on without glancing at her. He seemed suddenly distanced from her as if he had other, more important things on his mind than his friendship with Theodosius Koriakis.

'Did you hear what I said?' she persisted when he made no reply.

'Yes, I'm sorry. My mind was elsewhere. Yes, Theo and I are good friends.'

She opened her mouth to ask more but he suddenly cut her off before she could utter a word.

'Zoe, why don't you snatch some shut-eye? It's going to be a long journey and you must get some rest.'

'We're nearly at the marina,' she protested, and that strange feeling of apprehension was back with her again.

'We're not going to the marina. We're picking up a boat from the other side of the island.'

'But I thought——'

'You thought we were using Theo's yacht; sorry to disappoint you but he's having some work done on it and we're hiring another.'

He was lying, or else Theo had lied about the work on the yacht. The refurbishing had been completed months ago.

Zoe sat back and closed her eyes, squeezed them tight because apprehension had curdled to a fear. She wasn't sure if she was actually afraid of Franc or it was something else. There wasn't anything to be afraid of, but nevertheless her stomach had tightened into a tight ball.

She licked her lips and tried to relax and not be silly, but something wasn't quite right—no, not right at all.

CHAPTER THREE

THE yacht to take them to the mainland wasn't one Zoe recognised. She knew every one on the island. The jetty belonged to a friend of Theo's who was away in Turkey on business. She glanced up at the villa that sprawled beyond the beach, for some reason seeking some reassurance that all was well. She saw no one.

Franc helped her aboard. Relief swamped her as she saw there was a crew, though she knew none of them.

'Whose yacht is this?' she asked Franc as they went below to the cool, air-conditioned lounge.

'Not mine, sadly.' Franc smiled and suddenly she did feel safe, and yet that was a strange feeling in itself. Why had she been afraid in the first place?

He went off to get coffee as they pulled away from the jetty and she realised he hadn't answered her query. She shrugged and sprawled out on the sofa, grateful for the coolness.

'Is this a mystery tour?' she asked him when he came back with the welcome coffee.

'No, you know you're on your way to Athens; I've already told you that.' He poured the coffee and asked her if she wanted cream or milk.

She shook her head. 'Thick, black and very sweet,' she told him. 'But I don't know where after Athens. I've no passport with me, you

47

know...nothing, come to that,' she murmured half to herself.

'We're not going anywhere where you'll need your passport.'

'Or any clothes,' she added. 'I find this all very mysterious.' Odd, but she felt a buzz of reluctant excitement too. She was going to work for Franc Blakemore, destination unknown, and without a stitch of clothing to her name apart from the white cotton jeans and raspberry silk shirt she was wearing! But suddenly it wasn't very exciting at all. She swung her legs to the deck.

'Look, Franc, this is all very peculiar——'

He reached out and touched her arm to reassure her, giving her a warm smile. 'I'm a pretty peculiar guy, Zoe; you'll find that out soon enough. I do things in my own mysterious way; it's necessary in my job. Trust me, though, and don't look for any problems, because there aren't any.'

She frowned at him. 'But there are. I haven't any clothes!'

'They are already there——'

'Where?' she blurted. 'Where is *there*?'

He sighed and lifted his coffee. '*There* is a tiny island, north of Paradise, south of Utopia. It has no name, no one lives there, no one passes there, no one knows it's there.'

Zoe laughed hesitantly. 'Don't be silly. You're trying to frighten me.'

'Why should an uninhabited island frighten you?'

She watched him drink his coffee before attempting to answer that one. Confusion dulled her brain for a few seconds. Why this apprehension again?

'It . . . it doesn't . . . but——'

'You're not afraid of me, are you?'

Her cheeks burned and she gulped at her coffee. More afraid of herself than anything. An isolated island that no one knew about, with Franc Blakemore her only company? He didn't know it but this was all so very cruel.

'Have I reason to be afraid of you?' Her eyes locked into his—very bravely, she thought.

He shook his head. 'None whatsoever. We know each other far too intimately for there to be any fear.'

Ah, perhaps that was the problem. 'But I . . . but I might be afraid of you . . . if . . . if you tried . . .'

'If I tried to make love to you again?' He grinned and placed his coffee-cup carefully back in the saucer. 'I *will* make love to you, Zoe, and you know it. You can only fear something if you are desperate for it not to happen, and the only desperation you will show will be to know how soon it will happen after we arrive.'

'Don't be so damned arrogant!' she hissed.

'It's not arrogance, sweet one; I know it to be a certainty. I'm honest; why can't you be?'

'Honest about what?' she wailed.

'About what you want.'

'I want to know a million things, none of which is remotely related to sex.'

'We were discussing sex,' Franc insisted with a teasing gleam to his eye.

'I wasn't!' Zoe pouted.

Franc raised a dark brow. 'There you go again, denying, running, avoiding.' He stood up and stretched. 'Little chance of that when we arrive on our island.' He bent over her and planted a soft kiss on her brow. 'No reason to deny, nowhere to run to, no chance of avoidance.'

'Another prison?' Zoe retorted as he reached the door to the upper deck.

'It will be whatever you care to make of it, Zoe. It's all up to you. I have every intention of having a damned good time.'

'And what about the work we're supposed to be going to do?' she thrust at him as he turned away.

He was smiling as he swivelled back to face her. 'That's exactly what I meant—work. It's my turn-on. What's yours?'

'I haven't found it yet,' she sparked back, 'but I suspect it might take the form of the slow poisoning of a certain legend in his own right.'

Franc laughed. 'Theo did say you were a rotten cook; perhaps I'd better take over the culinary duties while you stick to what you do best...' He said the last word in Greek, causing a flush of embarrassment and fury to engulf her.

Zoe bunched a serviette and flung it at him, a puerile attempt to show her fury. He just laughed once again and left her to coil herself on the sofa and sulk.

By the time they reached Athens Zoe was distinctly bemused. On the yacht trip she had dozed in a stupor and couldn't shake off this feeling of sloppy languor. It was hot, of course, but she was used to it. Her head felt frothy and her limbs dragged, and the switch from one taxi to another to the airport seemed to be a ridiculous waste of time.

'How did you get such rapid clearance?' she asked Franc as he helped her into the gleaming islander aircraft that was already throbbing its engines. 'Not even Theo gets through that quickly.'

'I know the right people in the right places.'

'So does Theo.'

Franc buckled her seatbelt for her and glanced at his watch as he replied. 'We swim in different streams, though. In this situation I would get priority over a shipping magnate.'

'Huh! And what situation would that be?' The froth in her head was clearing and she was beginning to think straight. 'This is hardly a life-and-death situation, and in spite of what you do for a living you're not James Bond, you know.'

He didn't answer her question. He seemed distracted, not quite with her. That apprehension coiled again and she dismissed it by concentrating her thoughts solely on the looks of the man who was now up front speaking to the pilot. He was very striking, all man, dark and interesting, a head-turner. She wondered if he made love with all his mistresses the way he had loved her. It hurt to think about it but it helped too. She had been one of a number and she would have to keep reminding herself of that if she wanted to avoid another big mistake in her life.

She frowned. What had he meant by getting priority over a shipping magnate in this situation? She wanted him back here to ask, but he was having what seemed like a very concerned conversation with the pilot.

'So whose plane is this?' she asked when he came back to sit next to her.

'Not mine, sadly,' he repeated as if that was his stock phrase for every query about his private life.

'Is anything yours? I mean, do you actually own anything apart from an enormous ego?' He ignored the insult, though with his ego he probably took it as a compliment, not an insult.

'Possessions, you mean?'

'Yes, possessions. A home or homes, your own aircraft, your own yacht, a car. They say you earn mega-dollars for your security services, so what do you spend it on?'

He shrugged his broad shoulders as the engines roared and they taxied down the runway. 'Knowing what I know about security has probably made me insecure. Life and possessions are very ephemeral. I hire whatever I need—homes, yachts, aircraft.'

'Women?'

'Never women,' he said, mock gravely. 'They come gift-wrapped in black silk and are delivered to my bedroom.'

Zoe flushed deeply at that reminder. 'So where do you actually live?' she persisted.

'Wherever I rest my head.' And he proceeded to do just that; rest his head back against the head-rest and close his eyes.

Zoe did likewise. So he was very secretive about his personal life, but perhaps he had to be. He advised the most important and eminent people in the world on their security. A man in that position could be a terrorist target himself. He probably knew where royalty kept their keys to their safes and where dictators kept their mistresses.

Zoe shifted uncomfortably in her seat. He probably lived his life on a knife-edge of tension, terrified of being kidnapped and tortured to near-death for all he knew. She opened one eye to glance at him. He didn't look easily scared, though, but nevertheless a man living like that would have no room in his life for a wife or children. Mistresses by the score, yes, but not a true love. Was that what Theo had hinted at? Blakemore looked no further because he didn't want a permanent woman in his life. She squeezed her eyes tight and tried to think of anything but that miserable thought.

'Wake up, Zoe.'

'Are we there?'

'No, not yet, but I want you to eat something. You've had nothing all day.'

'I'm not hungry.' She yawned. Her head was still a bit fuzzy and she had a raging thirst.

'Eat, Zoe.' Franc said it so firmly that she was suddenly very awake. He handed her a plate of delicious-looking smoked salmon sandwiches which she took without argument, realising she was very hungry after all.

'Tea or coffee?' he asked from the galley kitchen.

Zoe swivelled to look at him. 'Have you a cold drink? I'm very thirsty.'

'Sorry, this isn't the damned Hilton, you know,' he snapped. He looked tired and sounded on edge, and Zoe bit her lip.

'I'm sorry,' she murmured, and turned back to stare at the head-rest in front of her. The thrum of the engines irritated her, and so did he for snapping at her like that.

Suddenly she felt the top of her head being caressed and she jerked her head up.

'Sorry, sweet one. I didn't mean to bite at you like that. I made you tea; that will quench your thirst better than coffee.'

She took the mug from him and drank thirstily without looking at him. It tasted different but then he'd never made her a cup of tea before and his preference was probably for a stronger brew.

Zoe watched him take a drink to the pilot and then gazed round her at the interior of the plane. Some of the seats had been removed and there were two huge packing cases with ropes strapped round them. She wondered what they were and where they were going. She looked out of the window and only saw blue. Was it sea or sky? She wanted to go to the loo and stood, rather unsteadily.

'Are you OK?'

'Sure.' She smiled at Franc. 'I just want to freshen up.'

He took her elbow and helped her to the toilet. She felt like an old lady, and giggled.

'Don't lock the door, Zoe.' The order came through fog.

'Of course I won't,' she said meekly. She felt very warm and floaty inside. She looked at herself in the mirror and giggled again. There were no edges to her face. She looked all swimmy, her eyes large and liquid. Franc thought her beautiful. She was going away with him, somewhere warm, and he would love her and he would look after her, forever.

'Better now?'

She nodded and nearly fell across him as she tried to sit down again. He steadied her and brushed a wisp of her hair from her forehead as she slumped in her seat.

'Much further?' she asked dreamily.

'Nearly there, darling.' His voice was low and husky and coming from a long way away. 'Forgive me, beautiful one, dear God forgive me, but this is so very necessary.'

His mouth closed over hers and sealed his words in her heart forever. She lifted her heavy, heavy arms to slide around his neck. The kiss was the best, the only thing in her life that was whole and complete. Her lips parted and his mouth was so sweet and sensuous on hers. He was kissing her forever, loving her forever. He did love her. He had come back for her, hadn't he?

She felt his arms move at the back of her, a slight pressure on her shoulders. Weakly she moaned his name and tried to ease her shirt from her shoulders. Franc wanted to love her and she wanted to help him.

'I love you,' she murmured croakily in a voice that wasn't her own.

His mouth returned, more ardently than ever, then he moved away from her.

'Tell me that when we land, sweetheart.'

She felt cool air on her forehead and tried to open her eyes. She shouldn't be sleeping when Franc was trying to make love to her.

There was a noise in her ears, a shushing noise like rushing air. Franc was hauling her to her feet. She felt pressure between her legs.

'Franc?'

'Darling, it's all right, just a harness. It won't hurt you. Open your legs, Zoe!'

He was shouting at her now and the shushing sound was getting louder. Zoe struggled, lashed out, fought to clear her head. Oh, God, she couldn't see. Her eyelids were so heavy, she could hardly keep them open. She struggled, though, and widened them.

'Franc!' she cried. There was brightness all around her as if the plane was open. Dear God, it was! A gaping hole at the rear of the plane.

'Listen, Zoe, just listen to me!' Franc roared over the rushing sound. He gripped her shoulders fiercely. Her shoulders, they felt heavy, there was something on her head, there was something on her back, between her legs... Oh, no!

Franc shook her to her senses. 'Don't worry,' he shouted. 'I won't let you go. Look, I'm hooking us together. You're going to be all right.'

Shocked, she tried to focus her eyes on his hands as they fumbled with a clasp at her breast. The fuzziness was receding; she felt as if she was coming out of a coma and stepping into a living nightmare.

'What... what...?' Her words were spun from her mouth by terror as Franc lurched them both towards the gaping hole.

She fought, she struggled, she bit and screamed till her throat was raw. Then Franc's mouth closed over hers and stilled the screams and choked the life from her. She went limp and knew she was going to die, and it just wasn't fair.

'Now, Zoe, we are going now! When you feel the ground under your feet, buckle your knees, do you hear me? Buckle...'

'Don't be crazy...' She didn't finish, couldn't say that she would be dead before they hit the ground.

'Oh... my *God*!' she screamed as her feet trod— nothing!

Cold air hit her, crashed into her lungs, nearly burst them with the force. Her body was already dead, lifeless, swinging like a rag doll in Franc Blakemore's embrace. Her skin stretched like a death mask over her face and she buried it in his chest. Her stomach was everywhere but where it should be, her hair streamed loose from her helmet. Her eardrums pounded. Her fingers grasped desperately at anything she could find.

And then came a raw instant of unbelievable pain as the harness wrenched between her legs, jarring every bone in her body. She felt as if she was being sucked back into the plane they had just ejected from. Her chest hurt where the life-saving hook between them cut desperately into her.

Then a strange stillness and warmth in the air around her—the last death-throe. Her weightless legs came up instinctively and clasped around Franc's thighs and her breath came back in heart-rending sobs of sheer terror. She didn't want to die. She tried to open her eyes, partially succeeded, saw blue and more blue and then squeezed her lids tight again.

There was no noise but her heart thudding in her chest, no noise of the plane, nothing but that eerie thud, thud of her heart.

'For God's sake get your legs down, Zoe!' Franc roared, and then it was too late. There was a terrible thud as they hit the ground in an ungainly mass of struggling arms and legs and nylon ropes and wind and heat.

Zoe bit sand, gulped air, retched and panted for more air and then she felt billowing silk shroud all around her like angels' wings.

There was silence and more silence; she opened her eyes and prayed she was dead because she couldn't live with all her limbs twisted and broken. Her head hurt and she fumbled with the strap of her protective head gear and wrenched it from her head.

She felt for Franc, her Siamese twin, for the last nerve-racking seconds. He wasn't there and the clasp at her breast hung from its holster. She grasped at mountains of silk and wrenched it aside.

'Franc!' she screamed but no sound came from her mouth. Shock, she was in shock, struck dumb with terror, and would never talk again!

'Franc!' she screamed again, and those broken, twisted limbs got her to a kneeling position. She couldn't see for the parachute settling around her. She scrabbled furiously at it, bunching it into bundles and shoving it behind her as she crawled to freedom. When she emerged he would be lying in a crumpled heap, lifeless, unconscious, crippled for life because she hadn't let go.

Brilliant sunshine scored her eyes and she blinked against the light. On all fours she scrambled from the last of the silk parachute. Her head cleared and her heart pumped pure, cleansing blood to her veins.

Franc sat a few feet away on white, white sand, his arms clasping his knees. He was grinning from ear to ear.

'The beautiful butterfly emerges from her chrysalis,' he husked with amusement.

Zoe's eyes narrowed in desperate fury. She tried to lurch at him but she was still confined by the harness and the parachute. She remembered a film she had seen and punched at the clasp at her breast. The harness sprang open and she was free, and Franc raised his brows in admiration.

'Clever girl——'

'I'll clever girl you . . . you bastard!'

She lunged at him, catching him off balance. They rolled over in the sand, Zoe punching him feverishly, Franc battling to catch hold of her flaying hands.

'You . . . stinking . . . Yankee bastard . . .'

'English actually,' he huffed, grasping her wrists and rolling her over to spin her under him on the hot sand.

'You . . . English bastard, then!'

He straddled her, pinned her hands above her head and leaned down over her. He was still grinning at her.

'Remember what I said about swearing?'

'Don't you dare! Don't you dare come near me ever again. I hate you for that, Franc Blakemore, I hate you!'

He laughed. 'Before we jumped——'

'*I* didn't jump! I was dragged!'

'Don't split hairs, darling. Before we jumped you said you loved me——'

Zoe struggled under him helplessly, her memory returning to humiliate her. 'I said nothing of the sort! Don't be so stupid! I couldn't love a maniac like you!'

'But you said—a little slurred maybe, but I definitely got the words—"I love you."' He lowered his head as if intending to kiss her but Zoe twisted her head to one side and squeezed shut her eyes.

'I didn't...I couldn't...have said that...' Her head spun. Oh, damn him, she had. Franc had been making love to her and she had said she loved him. But why had she murmured it? She must have been out of her mind. Her mind *had* been fuzzy.

'Oh, no!' She turned her face to his. He was inches away from her, smiling enigmatically down at her. 'You didn't,' she husked incredulously. 'You couldn't have——'

'A mild sedative, Zoe. It was necessary——'

'You drugged me!' she screamed, struggling more than ever, so desperately that he unstraddled himself from her and let her sit up. He gripped her shoulders to hold her steady.

'It was only a mild sedative, in your coffee on the boat, in your tea on the plane.' He was still laughing and it infuriated her more.

'Twice? You drugged me twice?' She couldn't believe this. He was joking surely? But she had been rather dazed on the earlier part of the trip and she definitely was muzzy on the plane. 'But...but I could have died,' she cried plaintively. 'I could have died, Franc Blakemore!' Her voice rose hysterically and Franc shook her slightly.

'I needed your full compliance to make that jump, Zoe. If you hadn't been sedated you could have seriously hurt yourself.'

'You are crazy!' she spat trying to scrabble to her feet. Franc released her and she towered over him, swaying only very slightly. Her limbs weren't broken, no thanks to him! 'You *are* a lunatic! You can't just go around pumping drugs into people. It's dangerous, damned dangerous!'

'I know your full medical history, Zoe, and the sedative——'

'My full medical history? What sort of weirdo are you, for heaven's sake?'

He looked up at her, squinting his eyes against the sun. 'It was necessary, in case of emergencies. We could be here a long time and if you fell sick——'

'I won't fall sick,' she spiked back at him. 'And if I did you're the last person I'd ask for medical advice ... What are you talking about—we could be here a long time?' Her head was reeling again and she longed to sink back down to that warm, soft sand. Her hand came up to her brow.

'Are you all right?'

She raised her chin bravely. 'Perfectly all right. Now would you kindly tell me what all this is about? Couldn't we have landed here in a more conventional way, a *saner* way?'

'No landing strip,' he said nonchalantly, easing up to his feet and brushing sand from his jeans. Zoe passed him on her way down. She fell to her knees and would have fallen flat on her face in the sand if Franc hadn't scooped her up into his arms. She clung to him as he carried her up the beach and gently deposited her in the shade of an outcrop of volcanic rock.

'Thirsty?' he asked gently.

She nodded. Thirsty and very confused.

For the first time Zoe gazed around her. The swimming and shushing in her head was going away. She saw white sand and bright pale sky and sea that shimmered forever in every direction. There was no sight of any other islands. Hadn't Franc said no one passed here?

The huge packing cases she had seen on the plane were lying on the beach, sunk deep into the sand with the impact of the drop, their parachutes lying lifelessly across them. Zoe shuddered. Dear God, she had jumped out of a moving plane with Franc Blakemore! If she had known...

There was no sign of Franc till she swivelled round and saw a rough white stone building on the edge of the beach, shaded and almost concealed by citrus trees. He was coming out of the open doorway carrying a bottle of water. If he'd been carrying a bottle of Dom Pérignon she couldn't have been more surprised.

She drank thirstily and Franc, who had sank down in the sand next to her, watched her. When she had finished she ground the base of the bottle into the sand but said nothing.

'Still mad at me?' Franc said quietly.

Zoe nodded, and suddenly she wanted to cry, for a few hundred reasons. Shock at the unexpected arrival at this place, horror at what Franc had done to get her here, and dismay at what she had admitted to him under the influence of that wretched sedative.

'I had to do it, Zoe. I know you well enough to know you would have fought to the death rather than have jump voluntarily out of that plane.'

'You don't know me at all,' she whispered. 'You had no right to put me in such danger. If Theo knew——'

'Theo does, and though he wasn't very happy he trusted me enough to get you here safely. Now look

at us both, completely unscathed by our experience;
but it could have been very dif-
ferent——'

'Yes, it needn't have happened at all! Why,
Franc? Why all this performance to get here? A
parachute jump of all things. Why? Why? Why?'

'I've told you, there isn't a landing strip here.'

'Why fly? Why not come all the way by yacht?'
She raked her hands through her tangled mass of
hair. Apprehension again; it tingled her spine and
the back of her neck.

'It was too far to come by sea.' He reached out
a hand and she took it and got to her feet. He didn't
let go of her hand but held it gently. 'It was the
only way to get us here, Zoe. Now I promised you
there were no problems, and there aren't. You must
trust me——'

'After this I'll never trust you again as long as I
have a nose on my face!' She snatched her hand
out of his. 'You dope me into a stupor, throw me
out of a moving plane . . .' She kicked the bottle at
her feet. 'What was in that? Hydrochloric acid?'
She suddenly clutched at her stomach. Was she out
of her mind? She had drunk it without thinking.

Franc laughed. 'What sort of an accusation is
that to make to the man you love?'

'Love!' she spat as if the very word were poison.
'I don't love you. I might have said it but don't
forget I was under the influence.' She suddenly
smiled. 'Or maybe I was just thinking of someone
else at the time. Yes, that was probably it. I was
thinking of Pierre, just as I was thinking of him
that night in Switzerland——'

He hauled her into his arms and held her tightly, his hot breath fanning her cheeks. 'And who's holding you now, Zoe, sweet one?' She detected a deep underlying anger to his grated question and for a brief second wondered at it. Then his mouth crushed her lips and his body locked into hers, melding her every aching muscle into the power of his.

The sexual flow nearly devastated her and liquid fire finished her off as it snaked through every vein of her body. Even now, bruised and weary, travel-torn and still fuzzy from the whole experience of those last mind-numbing minutes, she wanted him to love her. He had done terrible things to her this day and if he said the right words now she would forgive him everything; but for what? A few hours or weeks or maybe months of loving and then nothing, because she was on loan to him, and goods borrowed had to be returned.

She drew her mouth from his, desperately, reluctantly, but it had to be done.

He made no attempt to kiss her again, just gazed down into her liquid brown eyes. His hands came up and smoothed her tangled hair from her face, a gesture so tender and caring that she nearly weakened. But there was a grim determination in his steely eyes and his jaw was tense.

'Don't ever think of another man when we make love again, and don't ever throw another lover's name in my face. Remember that, Zoe, when your body cries out for release. On this island of ours there's only Franc Blakemore on call, night and day.'

Zoe drew in an agonised breath. 'I'll...I'll never call out for you...'

'You say that now because you're still mad at me, but you will cry out for me; yet I might get impatient waiting and call for you first. Then what will you do, Zoe?' His tone dripped mockery.

'Go deaf!' she retorted hotly. *Just as I went blind when I believed I really loved you,* she thought to herself.

'I'll just have to call extra loud, then, won't I?' His hand came up and brushed over her crumpled silk shirt, smoothed against her breasts, trailing white-hot fire over her skin beneath. 'Is that loud enough for you?'

She tensed her whole body. How easily he had got the message. The heat of her skin was enough for him to know. She raised a hand and gripped his wrist, drawing it away from her breast. She smiled up at him.

'I beg your pardon? I didn't quite catch that,' she uttered insolently.

She knew he was going to laugh, and turned away; that was something she definitely didn't want to hear.

CHAPTER FOUR

ZOE made her way up the beach to the rough stone building. The island was small and surprisingly fertile, but surely they weren't going to work here? It was primitive, without electricity. Oh, why were they here? Franc had wanted her secretarial services, not some castaway companion.

The old building was little more than a storeroom, stacked with provisions. There were cases of tinned goods, bottled water, gas bottles.

She turned as Franc's frame in the open doorway blocked out the light for a second.

'What are we doing here, Franc Blakemore?' she husked.

'We're going to work.'

'So you keep telling me, but why here and why not somewhere civilised?'

He took a while to answer as if deliberating, then he took a knife from his pocket and slit open one of the cases. 'I needed isolation,' he said at last. 'Theo knew of this island and decided it was ideal.'

'Ideal for what, balancing the books?' she retorted cryptically. 'Well, I don't believe you. I think this whole set-up is very odd, very peculiar indeed.'

'I told you I was a pretty peculiar——'

'Not good enough, Franc,' Zoe interrupted. 'Eccentricity is no excuse for all this.' She waved her hands at the boxes and cartons. 'How did all this get here? Not by parachute, I bet. There's enough for a siege. A boat must have brought this. Why couldn't *we* get here by boat?'

'This stuff was brought here weeks ago and there was no boat coming this way this time.'

'No!' Zoe cried, almost stamping her foot with impatience. 'I'm not going to accept that——'

'Well, you'll just have to!' Franc suddenly blazed, waving the knife at her. 'Now listen to me. I'm hungry and tired and these last few weeks of my life have been hell. All I want to do is get all this stuff sorted out without you bending my ears with your plaintive cries of why, why, why?'

'Answer me, then; just give me some answers to some very simple questions——'

'OK.' He stabbed the knife into a cardboard case. 'I'm winding my company up, copping out if you like. Another agency is taking over my clients and because of the highly confidential nature of my work I need total isolation, total peace and quiet to get it all sorted out. I want no interruptions, no outside influences to——'

'Winding your company up?' Zoe interrupted with a gasp. 'You said it was your turn-on.' She couldn't believe this. He was too young to retire, surely? How old was he? About thirty-four or five? She didn't know. She'd loved him for three years and didn't even know his age.

His eyes met hers and held them, and said slowly, 'Nothing stays the same forever.' She wondered if there was an underlying message to that. He proceeded to tear open the box. 'Do you feel well enough to give me a hand?'

'Is that it—all I'm going to get from you?' she persisted.

'There isn't any more, Zoe.'

'There is, oceans more,' she snapped. 'You haven't been around for three years and suddenly you appear at Theo's party—— '

'As an old friend and business associate I was included on the birthday guest list, nothing mysterious about that.'

'I didn't say there was anything mysterious about it but, now you come to mention it, it is more mysterious than peculiar.'

Franc grinned and shook his head in disbelief. 'You are quite determined to make something out of all this, aren't you? What a dull life you must lead.'

'I do not lead a dull life and I'm not looking to make a fantasy out of all this, but you haven't been very fair to me. I was bustled out of the villa this morning with no chance to pack, drugged and—— '

'Please, Zoe,' he interrupted wearily. 'I don't want to hear all those accusations again.'

Zoe opened her mouth to protest but closed it again. He was tired; she could see it now in the deep furrows of his brow. She crossed the room and stood by the box he was rifling through. He looked up and smiled at her.

'It all happened so quickly,' she told him quietly. 'I'm confused.'

'It happens that way sometimes,' he murmured, and she looked deep into his dark eyes to try and read what exactly he meant by that. She knew in her heart what she wanted to believe—that he was referring to love; but he wasn't, of course. 'Theo knew my plans,' he went on, 'and when I said I wanted to get away for a while and could do with the services of a good secretary—well, it all fell into place. Theo said he'd worked you too hard lately and you'd been tied to the villa and needed a break, and that was it. I took what was offered; it co-incided with his birthday party and you know the rest.'

Zoe knew nothing. Theo had led her to believe Franc had specifically asked for her. She was even more confused than ever.

'And nobody asked me what I wanted,' Zoe said with a sigh.

'And if you had been asked, what would you have said?'

Was he serious or not? Was he testing her or not? Did he really care whether she would have come here willingly or not? She would have followed him to the ends of the earth and not been afraid to admit it if she knew he was powered by the same feelings as she was.

'Theo controls my life. I do as he says. I have no choice.'

'One day you will have. One day you will marry and be free.'

'Huh—if any man can get past Theodosius Koriakis.' She went to the door and stood gazing down the beach to the water gently frothing on the shoreline. One man had got past Theo—this man Franc Blakemore, but he hadn't marriage in mind; he just wanted to 'borrow' for a while.

She let out a ragged sigh. 'Are the tents in those packing cases on the beach?'

He laughed behind her and put his hands to her waist to move her out of the doorway.

'No tents.'

'So we're camping down in here, are we?' she drawled sarcastically. She wouldn't put anything past this man.

His hand slid to hers and he pulled her gently away from the rough stone building. 'Peculiar I might be, but I do it in style. Come, let me show you where we will be living and loving.' He pulled her to a flat stone path that led through the citrus grove.

'Working and warring, don't you mean?'

'That's entirely up to you. You can make this trip pleasurable or not.'

'Depending on how you get your kicks,' she told him tightly, extricating her hot hand from his.

'I seem to remember how you get yours.'

'Well, I can't bring yours to mind for the life of me.'

'I'll remind you tonight when the sun goes down.'

'When the sun goes down tonight I go down with it,' Zoe yawned.

'And you rise with the dawn? So do I—that should be interesting,' he cut back suggestively.

Zoe flushed, swept her hair impatiently from her face and followed him along the track into the interior of the island.

It *was* a small island. A white-washed villa with an ochre tiled roof sat at the end of the citrus grove. You could just see the beach and the shoreline through the orange trees. Beyond the villa at the back was a small wooded area that ended rather abruptly. The sound of the sea came from that direction as if the water was coursing over a reef.

To the left and right of the villa the land rose and fell. There were outcrops of tawny-coloured rock and patches of dense greenery. It was lush and at the same time coarse and rugged.

'Is this one of Theo's islands?' She thought she knew them all, but not this one. She wished she knew how long she had slept on the flight, because then she could judge where they were. She could see no major coastline in the heat-hazed distance but that wasn't necessarily an indication of their isolation from civilisation. As the sun went down all manner of shapes could materialise out of the cooling horizon. She hoped some would tonight. She wanted assurance that the rest of the world wasn't so very far away.

'A friend of his, I believe.'

There was a wide terracotta-tiled terrace at the front of the villa and there were sun-bleached, rickety chairs and a table in the shade of a shadowy olive tree. The windows of the villa were small, the front door gnarled and sun-beaten. It looked like the rustic home of someone who had farmed the land and been beaten back by the savage weather that could sometimes rampage through the islands.

Zoe stood on the terrace, almost afraid to step inside. She'd seen many of these primitive-type dwellings on her travels round the Archipelago, but she'd never wanted to live in one.

'It's hardly the Parthenon in its heyday,' Franc said apologetically. He pushed open the wide wooden door. 'But it's cool and will suffice.'

Zoe was surprised when she stepped straight into the kitchen. It was big and airy and though far from being streamlined was pleasantly civilised. It had a

cooker and a fridge, all powered by bottled gas,
and a deep porcelain sink. It was furnished simply
with a good, strong, weathered pine table and chairs
that sat well on clean, polished terracotta tiles.
There were three steep steps down to a sitting-
room—a long, narrow room, heavily beamed with
an open fireplace to one of the long walls. This
room too was pleasantly furnished. Huge Turkish
cushions were plumped on a raised dais at one end
and there were brick bookshelves, a desk and a
chair.

'The bedrooms are through that door at the end,'
Franc told her. 'You explore while I start to bring
some of the stuff up from the beach.'

'I'll help,' she said quickly. She didn't want to
explore the bedrooms but . . . but surely better on
her own than with him watching her every
movement? 'After I've looked around,' she added
breathlessly.

'Have fun.' He smiled, that all-knowing smile of
his that raised the hairs on the back of her neck.

She waited till he had gone before she moved.
She still couldn't shake off this feeling of apprehension. It came and went, but each time it returned it seemed to be for a different reason. At
first she had been afraid for her feelings. Loving
him was worrying, then her fear had been for this
trip. It had been so rushed and then that hor-
rendous parachute jump, and now this place, so
very far from civilisation, such a strange place to
wind up a company.

Slowly she went to the far door and opened it.
There was a spacious inner hall with several doors
opening off from it. One was a ceramic-tiled

bathroom with everything anyone would need for living here permanently. There were two double bedrooms, both cool and quite dark because of the narrow windows to keep out the heat. Two bedrooms—thank heavens for that.

One of the rooms had some clothes hanging in an old wooden wardrobe. Zoe examined them. They were her size but nothing she recognised. There were shorts and skimpy tops, a couple of bikinis, little else. Probably all she needed for a stay on this island. She frowned. All this must have been organised ages ago and yet Theo and Franc had only just thrown it at her. She sighed. Franc Blakemore certainly worked in mysterious ways.

There was a third door from the hallway but that was locked. Zoe went outside to see if she could look into the window but it was shuttered.

'One of the rooms is locked,' she told Franc as he heaved a box down on the kitchen table.

'So how many bedrooms can you sleep in at once?'

She shrugged and proceeded to unpack cans of food, evaporated milk, vegetables and fruit. 'I just thought it odd.'

'Nothing is odd, Zoe; stop trying to make a drama out of all this. It's probably stuffed full of the owner's personal stuff. This is probably a vacation let.'

'A vacation let? I can just see your average bucket-and-spade family parachuting in here——'

'There is a boat——'

'You said nothing passes here.'

'Don't you ever forget anything I say?'

'I have a video memory.'

'So you must remember that I asked you to trust me and that there were no problems. Now why can't you just settle down?'

'I'm highly strung,' she bit back. 'Didn't you find that out when you went through my medical records?'

'Your personal idiosyncrasies are not stated in your medical history, but Theo did warn me about your occasional hysteria and that was why I sedated you before the jump. Now why don't you stop hassling me before——?'

'You give me another draught to keep me quiet?'

He stopped stacking the tins on the shelves and turned to her. 'I can think of a far more potent way of shutting you up. Would you care to go for it?' His eyes were hooded and threatening and she knew exactly what he meant.

'Consider me well and truly shut up,' she told him flintily.

'Pity,' she heard him mutter under his breath.

It took two more hot, grinding hours to bring the supplies to the villa. Franc suggested she stay in the cool and just unpack the stuff as he brought it from the store house, but she insisted on doing her fair share. She was feeling better, her head clearing.

'Are those clothes in the wardrobe for me?' she asked. She'd made tea while Franc was making the last trip and as he came into the kitchen she poured him a mug.

'Well, they're certainly not for me,' he grinned.

'Very funny,' Zoe breathed resignedly.

'They're nothing special but they'll do for here.' He sat down at the table and scored his wet hair

from his brow. He'd stripped down to the waist
and he glistened with sweat which matted the hairs
to his tanned chest.

Zoe couldn't wrench her eyes away from him.
She had loved and adored that body, once known
every inch of it intimately, and yet she knew so little
about him.

Her eyes flickered back to his face and he was
staring down at the wood grain of the table. He
hadn't seen her perusal of him, but she had the
feeling he had sensed it. When he did look up she
felt sure she had been right. He smiled and parted
his lips to speak and she tensed in anticipation of
some mocking comment from him.

'Why don't you go and shower? You look
exhausted.'

'So do you,' she murmured, her tension easing.
'Is there water in the bathroom?'

He nodded. 'I haven't fixed the pump from the
underground spring yet but the header tank on the
roof is full of rain water. The sun will have warmed
it but if you want a hotter shower you'll have to
wait till I've connected up the solar panels, and that
won't be till tomorrow.'

'Is there much more to bring up from the store?'

'Only the crates we dropped from the plane. You
get your shower and I'll deal with them.'

'No, I'll help.'

'I can manage.' He said it curtly and Zoe wondered why, but she was too tired to argue.

'I'd better make us something to eat, then. It will
be dark soon.'

'Get your shower. We'll worry about food later.'
He stood up and went out of the door and Zoe

wondered where he got his strength from. Hours ago he had said he was tired and hungry and now he was still going strong whereas she was nearly on her knees with exhaustion.

She pushed herself to open some cans before taking her shower. She couldn't let him do everything. She tipped a can of goulash and a can of potatoes into a dish, lit the oven and set it on low before going to take a shower.

The bathroom had a walk-in shower, and shampoo and toiletries were arranged on a shelf near by. Zoe slid out of her grimy jeans and shirt and stepped under the warm, soft spray. It was all she could do to keep her eyes open as the water trickled over her, lulling her, tempting her, relaxing her. But her mind ploughed on, lazily, but still asking questions. Why were clothes for her already here, these toiletries? She understood that she couldn't have parachuted down with her Vuitton suitcases strapped to her back, but why the parachute in the first place? Surely it would have been easier to have come by boat with the supplies? And Franc—why pick this place to get away from it all to fold up his company? He *was* peculiar.

She dried herself and knew she wasn't going to be able to join him for supper tonight. She crawled under the sheet on the bed, a clean, fresh, sweet sheet that somebody must have made up. No more questions, she sighed, and closed her eyes and dreamt she heard a voice and saw a light in the darkness and felt someone brush a kiss across her brow. She liked dreams like that.

*   *   *

Her bedroom door was wide open when she awoke, and she knew Franc must have been in her room. She remembered she had shut it quite firmly the night before. The dream was fading and all she could recall was the light. Had he come to her room expecting...? She shook herself awake and crawled out of bed.

She slumped back down again. Every muscle in her body was like perished elastic. She had no strength. The parachute jump. She'd probably tensed muscles she didn't know she owned in that terrifying leap.

'Now just imagine how you would have felt if you'd jumped sober.'

Franc walked straight into her room and placed a glass of freshly squeezed orange juice on the table by the bed. He was quite respectable in worn shorts and equally worn T-shirt whereas Zoe had just a second to cover her nakedness with the sheet before he was upon her.

'Point taken,' she said, ruefully rubbing her calf muscles under cover of the sheet. 'But one thing I'd like to bring up this morning—when you were busy collecting a wardrobe of clothes for me you failed to include a nightdress. Was that intentional or a mere oversight?'

'Intentional, I assure you. I find them an encumbrance, don't you?'

'You do, do you? Well, you did say you were a bit peculiar, but I wouldn't have thought wearing nighties was one of your peculiarities.'

'What wit first thing in the morning,' he drawled sarcastically. 'I missed it the first time around.'

Zoe inwardly grimaced at that cruel reminder of how she had crept out of his room that early morning in Switzerland while he slept.

'What were you doing in my room last night?' She wasn't sure he had been, but she was sure she had closed that door.

'Checking to see if you were all right.'

'Are you sure you weren't checking to see if I was waiting for you?'

He smiled. 'It did cross my mind, but you would have been unlucky, Zoe—virile I might be, but superhuman I'm not. After what we went through yesterday I'd have been no use to you whatsoever last night.'

How good he was at making her feel the wanton hussy, and how silly she was for falling into the trap every time; but at least he was honest about his capabilities, which was a surprise.

'Well, if you check me out in future, would you be so kind as to shut the door after you? I want my privacy.' She reached for the juice and drank it thirstily.

'For what? Or shouldn't I ask?'

'I like my privacy, I *demand* my privacy.'

He leaned over her and tweaked the edge of the sheet she was still clutching to her breast with one hand. 'There's no privacy here, Zoe, and no demands either. Closed doors are dangerous; leave yours open as I leave mine open.'

'And I don't need three guesses to know why!'

'All three would be wrong. Old habits die hard. In my line of business a closed door is asking for trouble when a quick escape route is needed.'

'Like fleeing from someone's bedroom where you shouldn't be? I suppose I should have guessed *that*!'

'You have quite a wicked mind at times,' he smiled, lifting the sheet up around her neck.

'Not wicked enough to leave bedroom doors open for you and not wicked enough to contemplate creeping into yours either.'

A dark brow went up and she knew what was coming. 'You've changed; once you were wicked enough for anything and everything.'

'Once I made a mistake,' she husked, trying to abort the rush of colour that was rising to her cheeks. 'Now leave me alone to dress and close the door after you. If you don't——'

'If I don't you'll have to get up and close it yourself, and I'm just across the hallway with *my* door open.' He strode across the room and paused in the doorway. 'I've never seen you naked. Strange, isn't it? After all we did that night we haven't actually seen each other in the flesh.'

She was grateful he didn't add a suggestion of how to rectify that, though the thought of what he might have suggested was enough to quicken the beat of her heart. She waited till she heard his step on the tiles in the sitting-room then she dragged her weary body out of bed and dressed in a pair of red shorts and matching top. Had he bought these? They fitted perfectly and were her favourite colour too.

Zoe spent the morning discovering the island, small and lush though it was. Franc was busying himself with the solar panels, but he warned her not to go too far.

'I don't think there is a "too far",' she retorted as she trod purposely towards the small pine wood behind the villa. Who did he think he was, warning her like that, as if she might try and escape? That apprehension again, tingling and tantalising at the small of her back. She felt like a prisoner. She *was* a prisoner, with him insisting she kept doors open so he could keep an eye on her, warning her not to wander too far.

She was right about the coral reef. There was one a few hundred yards out to sea and the sea swirled impatiently over it. The pine wood halted abruptly at the edge of the beach and there was only a small strip of sand to wander along to the furthest point of the island. This side of the island was savage and weather-beaten. A lot of the pines were nearly stripped bare of their branches and Zoe could imagine the storms that raged here at times. This side of the island would be unapproachable by boat, and for some reason Zoe shuddered. Suppose there was a storm or something happened to Franc—an injury or a snake bite; how would she get help for him?

It materialised before her eyes as if she had the power to activate her thoughts into real life. A long grey-green snake uncoiled from a pile of flotsam gathered on the beach and slowly moved towards her.

Zoe's first instinct was to scream but she caught the wayward plea in her throat and halted it. Any sudden movement and it might spring at her. But she couldn't just freeze here like a statue; it would sense her fear, attack before she had a chance to flee.

'Stay still, quite still,' Franc breathed behind her. His hands came round her waist and for a wonderful moment she thought he was going to swing her out of the slow, slithery path of the approaching snake, but his hands caressed and a new fear sprang in her heart.

Gently he drew her back against him and his mouth nuzzled the back of her neck.

Zoe's eyes were wide and transfixed and never left the snake, which had halted now, its head raised as if in curiosity.

'What....?

'Shush,' husked Franc. She felt every hardened muscle of his body pressed into her back; his arms around her tightened and then moved as languorously as the snake had slithered towards her, down over her hips, lower and lower to her groin. The snake had lost interest now and was coiling away from them, but there was a new danger—a new danger in the form of Franc Blakemore.

He held her so firmly that she had no hope of struggling out of his arms, and yet in that mixed moment of relief that the snake wasn't going to strike she almost welcomed his caress.

Her whole body sagged for a second and he took advantage of her compliance by gently turning her into his arms.

His arousal shocked her and her mouth parted, giving him yet another advantage over her. His mouth was impassioned and a gasp grazed in her throat. The bare flesh of his thighs pressed into hers and the effect on her nerve-endings was catastrophic. She didn't want this—this dangerous, delicious contact, her reasoning told her, but her heart cried out something else: that she wanted him more than ever, that she would always want him.

He drew her harder into him, moving against her so languidly that the movement was scarcely a movement but more of a sensation. His hands seemed to cover every inch of her in his leisurely caress. His mouth grazed her lips, her chin, the hot, silky skin of her throat.

He moved her top aside and drew his lips across the perfumed skin just above her inflamed breasts, and she knew if the thin cotton fabric gave enough and he made contact with her breasts everything would be lost.

'Please don't, Franc...I can't...'

His bruising mouth swept away her fevered protest as if it weren't worth any consideration, and it was then she realised that to him it probably wasn't. She was here for the taking just as she had been in Switzerland, and Franc Blakemore took what he wanted without fear. They were alone here, no one to witness, no one to run to, no escape.

She tore her mouth from his and her small fists bunched on his chest to prise him away from her.

'And why can't you?' he husked, reaching out and preventing her from sprinting away from him by gripping her shoulders.

'I should have said won't, not can't!' she blurted back at him. 'I *won't* let you make love to me again.'

'You make it sound so one-way, Zoe. When we made love all those years ago it was together, not me making love to you.'

Her eyes blazed bitterly. 'Stop it! I don't wish to be reminded of the biggest mistake of my life. I want to forget all that——'

'Forget it, then, and let's start afresh, though what difference it will make I can't see. We still desire each other as much as we ever did.'

'I don't desire you, but you are obviously having a struggle. You use every opportunity to touch me.' She heatedly waved her hand in the direction of where the snake had disappeared. 'That snake was going to attack me and yet all you could see was an opportunity to grab hold of me... and... and don't you dare laugh at me!'

Franc Blakemore dared; still holding on to her, he threw his dark head back and laughed out loud.

'It's not funny! It just isn't!'

Still laughing, he swivelled her round and, linking his arm around her shoulder, he directed her back through the pine wood to the villa. 'No, it isn't funny, but it is. You weren't to know the snake was harmless——'

'It looked lethal,' she spat back.

'If it were, you would have been prostrate on the sand, because snakes don't hesitate.'

'Like a certain other snake I know who isn't a million miles from me at this moment. You didn't hesitate either, *and* you nearly had me prostrate on the sand too.'

'Ah, but like that harmless little snake I didn't actually attack, I just put a smidgen of temptation your way. Were you tempted?'

She couldn't fault his honesty and openness, and that was a depressing thought. If he had any feelings for her whatsoever, he would openly say so; all he ever openly said was the truth—he desired her, full stop.

Zoe wasn't so open and honest with him. 'It takes a lot to tempt me, and that wasn't a lot.' She jerked her head to look up to him. 'And don't get any funny ideas about upping the pressure, because temptation is a weakness and that's one of your failings, not mine.'

'But it was once your failing too. You came to me like a lamb to the slaughter.' He sighed reflectively. 'The woman I made love to that night in Switzerland was a sweet and loving giver; she's changed. She's now wary and embittered.' No humour now. His voice was flat and unemotional.

They had reached the back of the villa and Zoe stopped in the shade and slowly turned to him. She was inexplicably hurt by that. If she was embittered the blame lay with him, though he could never know it, nor would ever know it. She had loved a stranger and suffered for it, and it was her problem, not his.

'The woman you made love to that night never existed,' she told him softly. 'She was a figment of both our imaginations.'

'I don't suffer from such flights of fancy, Zoe. What I held in my arms was warm flesh and blood, shy, nervous at first, all very endearing, and then that blossoming into a sensuality no other woman has matched for me since.'

The pain went on and on, just as he had gone on and on bedding women since that night. She couldn't even hate him for that because she was numb with pain.

'And you think you can pick up from where you left off?' She shook her head in defiance. 'Never, you'll never do that.'

His dark eyes riveted her to the spot. 'How can you be so positive of a sweeping statement like that?' The painful question came slowly and drily and confidently, as if the only answer could be her uncertainty.

It was Zoe's turn to laugh, a brittle cry that was painful to execute and deliver. 'Nice try, Franc Blakemore. Issue you with a challenge you can't fail to take up? No way; I don't trip over trick bricks like that.'

There was a bleak silence after that statement, so positive that Zoe could almost sink her teeth into it. Franc just stood watching her, as if searching her inner mind for some of that sensuality he had mentioned.

She couldn't be sure what he was thinking, but she had a good idea. He looked almost regretful, as if he had made a mistake in bringing her here. He had thought she would be as submissive as before and was now realising his mistake. So he made mistakes too; that gave her a certain gratification.

She tilted her chin. 'I suppose I'd better get some lunch; after all, I'm here to work, aren't I?' she questioned sarcastically.

Franc didn't answer that but simply turned away from her and the villa and set off through the citrus grove. She watched him go, feeling low and disgruntled and ashamed of herself. It was one time when his roar of laughter would have been welcome.

CHAPTER FIVE

'WHY can't I go swimming on my own?' Zoe bleated, rubbing fiercely at her forehead. A headache was imminent, a storm was imminent. She knew the signs. 'When this storm breaks we won't have a chance for a swim; the sea will be a boiling inferno, and I'm a boiling inferno *now*. I need a swim to cool off.'

'Take a cool shower, Zoe. The sea isn't fit to swim in safely at the moment,' Franc informed her, glowering at the paperwork on the kitchen table.

Zoe had suffered days of this—work, work, work; and when she did demand a break for a swim he insisted on accompanying her. In comparison Theo's restrictions were very lax; at least with him she had the privacy of a swim in the pool on her own, the privilege of being allowed to shut her bedroom door after her. Every night here she had shut her door only to find it gaping wide open when she awoke; well, tonight she was going to drag a chest of drawers across it, and then just let him try and get in!

'Where did you last live?' she snapped irritably, leaning over him to get his attention.

Wearily he looked up at her, his eyes dark and gaunt. It had been a miserable few days for him too, realising he had made a mistake in bringing her here; but she wouldn't allow him any sympathy. She was hating this as much as him. The tension between them was at shredding-point.

'London,' he breathed resignedly. 'Mayfair, to be precise. Am I permitted to ask why you need to know?'

She smiled sweetly. 'I just needed to prove a point. The Mediterranean and the Aegean don't lap up Park Lane, so what do you know about these waters? I've swum them all my life——'

Something snapped and Franc shot to his feet, the chair falling away behind him. 'OK, sweet one,' he grated, 'a swim it is!'

'On my own!' Zoe bleated as he manhandled her out of the kitchen, across the terrace and into the citrus grove. 'Can't I do anything on my own?'

'Nothing apart from your ablutions. I would have thought you would have got that through that pretty little head of yours by now.'

'Oh, yes, it's sunk in all right,' she argued, nearly stumbling on the exposed root of a lemon tree. 'I'm a prisoner here for some weird reason that only you and the maddest person in the world knows about. It's ten times worse than living with Theo, a million times worse than living with Satan!'

'You don't know when you're well off, Zoe.'

'This is well off, is it? By your standards maybe, but not mine.'

'You have standards, do you?'

'Meaning?' she blazed, skidding to a halt in a flurry of fine white sand.

He stretched out a long arm towards the frothing sea. 'Get in there before I toss you in by your ankles. You wanted this swim, so go for it.'

She pouted to infuriate him. 'Maybe I don't want it after all——' He snatched at her wrist and pulled her to the water's edge. 'But I've got my clothes on!' she screamed.

'So have I,' he grated bitingly. 'More washing for you tomorrow, but you did want this swim.'

'Not with my clothes on, you idiot!'

He waded in deeper and deeper, dragging her behind him. His wet shorts clung to his muscled thighs, and hers, of wispier fabric, flapped up around her groin. His soaking T-shirt, moulded to his broad chest and shoulders, enhanced his power whereas her clinging T-shirt, moulded wetly to her breasts, only exposed her raw sexuality. Oh, it couldn't have been worse if he had forced her to strip. She snatched her wrist from him and hugged her shoulders to conceal her breasts, hating him for this, hating him more than she had ever loved him.

Defiantly she struck out to sea, away from him and his threatening presence. His eyes had darkened when he had turned towards her and seen her small, firm breasts thrusting at the wet cotton; there was hungry desire in that look, and she didn't like what it did to her own ravaged senses.

He plunged after her as the first shuddering roll of thunder issued its first warning of what was to come. The sun was gone now, terrified from the skies by murderous black cloud.

Zoe felt the sea roll furiously under her and she knew she had been wrong to insist on a swim. Already the current was pulling at her legs. She turned to shout a warning to Franc, but he'd disappeared. Her eyes widened in terror. She was a strong swimmer, but was he?

She screamed his name, her head jerking wildly from side to side in search of some sign and then he surfaced next to her and she screamed his name once again—in relief this time, not blind terror.

'It's all right, don't panic, I've got you.' He took her strongly by her arms but she slithered out of his grasp.

'I'm...I'm not in...danger,' she spluttered, treading water and skimming wet hair from her face. 'I was...scared for you.'

'Flattered, I'm sure. Now let's get the hell back to shore before it's too late.'

He swam behind her protectively, and as Zoe struck her arms through the water her eyes filled with tears, warring with the salt water that was already burning them. He did care; he was looking out for her welfare and that was why he insisted on swimming with her every day—he cared so much for her that he was terrified to let her out of his sight.

Her bare feet made firm contact with turbulent sand but an angry wave lashed the back of her knees and she sprawled forward on all fours. Franc hauled her to her feet and she grasped at his arms for balance as the sea swirled around their calves. It was pouring with rain now and somewhere in the far distance lightning spurred the water, cracking furiously as the sea fought back.

The storm had broken and so had her tension. In that moment she wanted Franc to take her in his arms, for him to hold her and say that he cared and had been terrified for her life out there.

Her dream was about to be realised. He took her shoulders, but not in the caress she so longed for.

'Don't you ever put our lives in danger like that again!' he thundered, his voice matching that of the elements. 'You might see your life as worthless but I have a high price on my mine. When I tell you something I mean it. In future you will do as I say, because I know best. Have you got that?'

His harsh tirade hurt so badly that the only relief was to lash back at him. 'Oh, yes,' Zoe breathed scathingly. 'I've got it. You shout, I jump. I say yes, you say no. Whatever I say or do is wrong, wrong, wrong! If I lived to be a million I'd never do anything right by you——'

'Stop it, Zoe,' he warned in a voice tempered to calm her down.

'And don't speak to me that way—as if I were a child and you my keeper. I'm not a child, I'm a woman and . . . and . . .'

And she was a woman with needs, and at this moment she needed Franc. The feeling washed over her as the rain washed down her back. She was tired of fighting him, tired of looking for some sign that he might really care for her. She bit her lip in the realisation that he probably never would care for her. He didn't even desire her any more. Even his teasing and innuendoes had ground to a halt these past few days. God, but she had missed them.

'And what, Zoe?' he urged, his grey eyes still as thunderous as the leaden cloud above.

Water coursed from both their faces and the need to lift her hand and caress the water from his face was almost uncontrollable.

'And nothing,' she breathed hopelessly, her fists clenched at her side. She turned away from him and headed back to the villa.

*   *   *

The storm raged for the rest of the day and was still hammering around the island when Zoe started to cook the evening meal while Franc took a shower. Her headache was well established, aligned to the ache in her heart.

Their diet was limited. No fresh food, apart from oranges and lemons, only dried goods and whatever came out of a can. Tonight Zoe was cooking rice with a can of prepared pepperoni and tomato sauce. While the rice boiled she sipped bottled water and flicked through the file they had been working on today.

She couldn't believe Franc was serious about giving up his agency. He led such a varied and interesting life, but there was danger at every turn and she wondered if he was getting weary of forever looking behind him all the time. Though there was nothing in these routine files they were working on to indicate the knife-edge he worked on in some of the Middle East countries, he had hinted that his life had been threatened there several times. So was he suddenly running scared? Somehow Zoe couldn't imagine that, but something in his life had suddenly made him wary and wanting to get out.

'What do you intend doing with your life when you've passed over your agency?' she asked as he stepped up into the kitchen. He was clean-shaven, his hair damp, and he'd changed into battle-green cotton chinos and a black T-shirt. He looked every inch an SAS hero, but she knew him not to be. She had asked what sort of training he'd had to do the work he did, and though he had been a trifle evasive he had hotly denied the SAS.

'I think I'll grow potatoes,' he told her, lifting the lid and peering disappointedly into the pan of rice.

Zoe smiled. 'I'm sorry, I thought you liked rice.'

'Not three times a day.'

Zoe shrugged as he went to the fridge for water. 'I didn't arrange the supplies.'

'Yes, quite. How's your headache?'

'Thriving,' she told him.

'Have you taken anything for it?'

'You forget, I didn't have time to pack,' she told him sourly.

'Sorry, I'll get you something.'

The rice boiled over, hissing the gas out, and they both dashed for it, the sudden movement raging the pain to Zoe's head. She swayed and Franc frowned his concern as he rescued the rice pan and held it aloft still bubbling and hissing.

'Aspirins, top drawer next to my bed. I'll finish the dinner while you take it easy.'

For once she did as she was told and went obediently to find the aspirins.

His voice came like a rifle shot as she opened the drawer. The combined shock of her name being called so sharply, so warningly, and what she saw in the drawer had her reeling back against the bed as if she had been struck between the eyes.

'I'm sorry,' he offered gently, coming towards her. He had flown from the kitchen and was still wiping his hands on a tea-towel. The ludicrous comparison of him wiping his hands on a menial towel and what his hands were capable of doing with what she had seen in the drawer had her cringing away from him.

'I'm sorry,' he repeated, flinging the towel to the ground and stepping forward to slam shut the drawer. 'I'm sorry you had to see that.'

Zoe shook her head, shocked and bemused. 'But why?' she croaked in a cracked whisper.

Her husky question hung so long in the air that she despaired of it ever being answered.

'It's necessary,' he whispered back at last, so faintly that she wasn't even sure she had heard it. She stared at him, her mouth very dry, noting the sudden whiteness of his face. She guessed why he suddenly looked so sick and appalled. He had made a mistake; for once he had not been quite the legend he was renowned for. If someone else, a mortal enemy, had gone to that drawer and found that gun...

'Why...why is it necessary?' Zoe husked, her eyes wide and frightened. She had seen guns before. Theo's bodyguards and security men carried guns, most airport security guards carried guns; but this was somehow different—she wasn't sure why. Maybe it was finding the unexpected, maybe it had crashed home the fragility of this man's life, maybe it was the thought that it was completely unnecessary in this isolated island situation.

'I always carry a gun. It's a sad fact of life that it's necessary, but that's the way it is,' he told her grimly.

It was hardly an explanation and yet it was, and apparently all he was prepared to offer at the moment. He opened the drawer again and Zoe flinched in anticipation of him taking the gun out, but he only took out the aspirins and tossed the

packet to her. She caught it in both hands and stood
there clutching it fiercely.

'Take a couple and go and lie down,' he ordered
quietly. 'I'll call you when supper is ready.'

She moved stiffly away from the bed and to the
door. She wanted to reach out and touch him as
she passed him, to give him reassurance as well as
herself, but she wasn't sure why she wanted to do
it so she didn't.

She swallowed two aspirins with water from her
bedside carafe and lay on her bed staring up at the
ill-fitting beams breaking away from the clay tiles
of the roof. The rain lashed harder and harder till
the drone mesmerised her lids down over her eyes,
but she didn't sleep. Apprehension was an unwelcome guest once again.

'You're very quiet tonight,' Franc remarked as
they ate their supper in the kitchen. 'Is your
headache still troubling you?'

Zoe shook her head. 'No, it's gone.'

'What is it, then—the supper not to your liking,
or maybe my boring company is getting to you?'

She looked up at him quickly. 'You're not
boring.'

He smiled because he knew he wasn't. 'The
supper, then?'

She shook her head and gazed down at the rice
and pepperoni sauce. 'The supper is OK,' she
murmured.

There was a long pause and then Franc said
quietly. 'It's the gun, isn't it?'

She didn't want to look at him for fear of giving
her feelings away. While lying on her bed she had
thought and analysed why she had been so shocked.

The gun, lying there in his bedside drawer, probably loaded, had brought home to her his vulnerability. They said he was tough, a legend, a man with power and strength, but he would be a man useless in the face of a crazed terrorist pointing a gun at his head.

'Zoe?' Franc said softly, and reached across the table to tilt her chin. 'What's wrong?'

She desperately tried to stem the tears that were threatening to mist her eyes. She forced a smile. 'The gun shocked me,' she admitted weakly. 'It's not something you expect to find in a bedside-cabinet drawer.'

'You've grown up surrounded by high security. Theo's security men are armed——'

'I know, I know,' she interrupted quickly. It posed another thought—that Franc Blakemore the legend had probably advised those men to be armed—but she couldn't handle that thought as well. 'But why here? There isn't a threat to you on a deserted island in the middle of nowhere.'

'There isn't a corner of this world that isn't free from some sort of aggro——'

'Rubbish!' Zoe exploded, pushing her plate away. 'There is certainly no threat here, unless of course you consider me a threat.'

'Well, that's a possibility; you certainly know how to throw a few punches.'

'I've never struck you.'

'You beat the living daylights out of me the day we arrived here by parachute.'

Zoe couldn't help but smile at that. 'It was a nervous reaction, Franc. That was the worst, the most terrifying thing that has ever happened to me in my life.'

'I thought you were a natural at it, apart from the bit when you flung your legs around me. But on reflection it was very enjoyable, and feel free to repeat it any time you like.' There was humour back in his eyes and a teasing smile softened the corners of his mouth.

Zoe felt the tension ease from the back of her neck. He seemed more like his old self with his innuendoes, and she had never thought she would welcome it, but anything was better than thinking or talking about that gun.

Though when she went to bed later it all returned—the apprehension, the anxiety; but as she finally slipped into sleep her last thought was that something had changed, because she hadn't bothered closing her bedroom door.

'When this storm finally blows over I might try a spot of fishing to add a bit of variety to the diet.'

'Not for my benefit,' she told him as she poured freshly brewed coffee the next morning at breakfast. 'I love fish but I couldn't bear to cook them—all those slimy scales and squiggly innards.'

Franc grinned. 'I'll catch them, gut them and cook them; how does that grab you?'

'Not very enthusiastically, but if you could bake fresh, crusty bread that would really be something.'

He was laughing as he took his coffee and went to the open door to watch the rain still persistently falling. Zoe gazed at the back of his head and wondered what went on inside it. She wondered if he had noticed she had left her bedroom door open and what he'd thought of it. He hadn't interpreted it as an invitation, because he hadn't come to her, but had she meant it as one? She really wasn't sure.

'Is it my imagination or are we going over the same ground?' Zoe asked later. It was still raining and they had shifted to the sitting-room because the kitchen roof was leaking. Franc was seated at the desk and had brought a chair from the kitchen for Zoe.

'I'm sorry—this is very mundane paperwork, I know, but necessary nevertheless.'

Zoe couldn't see it, the necessity for all this checking and re-checking. If she had a computer all this could be done in an hour. She didn't understand Franc's need for such solitude either. If this was the winding up of his life's work he seemed very detached from it all. It was almost as if they were just plodding along, whiling away the hours and the days for want of something better to do.

Zoe was bored and restless, the rain getting her down, and there was something else that was troubling her. She didn't know how much longer she could go on living with him like this. Loving someone and not getting anything in return was wearing. She bit her lip; but what had she given him? Nothing but some of that aggro that was in every corner of the world.

'How long are we going to be here?' She couldn't see their work carrying them further than the end of the week.

'About a month.' It was the first time he had given her a definite time.

'All this will be finished by the end of the week,' she told him, not so much a protest as a statement of fact. 'Then what?'

He turned to her and the look in his eye was evidence of what he had in mind, and the flush to her neck started before he even opened his mouth to state it. But it was what she wanted, wasn't it? For him to desire her and want her . . . but no . . . not because there was nothing better to do.

She stood up quickly, hurried out of the room to the leaky kitchen, filled the kettle and slammed it on the gas, nervously striking match after damp match to ignite the jet. When it did ignite there was a whoosh and she stepped back jerkily.

'Take it easy,' came his voice from the steps. 'Never turn the jet on before you have the lighted match in your hand.'

'Shut up!' she breathed, clattering the mugs from the cupboard.

'Why so nervous? I never said a word, you know.'

'You didn't have to. I knew precisely what you were thinking,' she retorted.

'I doubt you'll ever know precisely what I think.'

'Huh! I should lose sleep over that!'

'You never lose sleep at night over anything, do you? Every night when I come to check you, you are sleeping the sleep of the dead,' he told her.

'Still checking up on me?' Zoe retorted, turning to look at him with dark eyes blazing. The thought of him coming to her room and her not knowing about it was infuriating.

'Last night you left your bedroom door open. What changed your mind, a surfeit of hormones?'

'If I had a surplus I wouldn't waste them on you!'

'Why the sudden subservience, then?' He took a lemon out of the bowl on the table and sliced it for their teas.

'I actually heeded your warning of yesterday—
do as you say because you know best.'

'That's progress, then—you are listening to what
I'm saying at last.'

'But not understanding most of it. Like being
here for a month, for instance. It isn't necessary,
it's not wanted by me——'

'But it's wanted by me,' he cut in sharply.

'Oh, and of course your word is the world's
command.' She waved a teaspoon at him. 'I tell
you something—if I had any means of getting off
this island I would. I don't even know why I'm here.
It's all...all so feeble. Your work could be done
by a cross-eyed, one-armed chimpanzee——'

'But they don't come so sexily packaged as you.'

Zoe fought the urge to tip his tea over his head.
'I'm not packaged sexily,' she told him wearily.
'You're just as bored and restless as I am.'

'There is a remedy for that.'

'And I don't need to be Einstein to work out what
that is!'

'Got it in one. We'll get down to it after this tea,
then,' he said.

Zoe nearly dropped the mug of tea she was about
to hand him. He took it from her hand before she
spilled it.

'Nothing less than a four-letter word and no col-
loquialisms; I like to play it straight,' he added.

'P-play it straight?' She saw the glint of mockery
in his eyes then and her heart stopped pounding
and steeled.

He shrugged. 'Scrabble, of course; what did you
think I meant?'

Her fingers tightened around her mug. Mercifully the rain had stopped, and though the wind was gusty it looked bright and wholesome out there. She wasn't going to share any more air space with him. She marched to the door and was about to step outside when she heard a sound, the drone of an aircraft, flying low.

She saw no sight of it because before she could look up she was flung back against the stone wall of the kitchen, the mug of tea went flying and Franc was pinning her there with the weight of his body. He kicked shut the open door and then there was stillness.

Startled, she froze, too shocked to move, too weighted by his muscled body tensed against hers. The drone went on and it was the only sound but for Franc's laboured breathing fanning the side of her head and his heart against her breast, his heart thudding so thunderously that her own stilled and merely fluttered helplessly under her ribcage.

Zoe held her breath though her mind raced hectically. Franc didn't move, just crushed her against the wall, his whole body tensed to rock-hardness. The urgency of the impact warned her not to move or speak.

The plane droned on, seemingly reluctant to leave the area, as if searching...

Zoe went ice-cold all over and in that moment she knew all there was to know. The gun, the isolation here, the secrecy in getting here. No one parachuted on to an island unless he or she had something to hide. Franc was hiding. His life was in danger, threatened. She mouthed a silent 'no' and squeezed tight her eyes. It seemed to be hours before the drone of the engines receded into the distance, but even when the silence folded comfortingly around them Franc didn't move away from her.

Slowly, painfully, Zoe opened her eyes and looked up at his face. It was pale and gaunt and she watched in silence as slowly his colour returned and the tension drained, leaving him looking exhausted. She knew and understood now. No man could live like this all his life, his very existence ever threatened. If you didn't get killed, the stress of anticipation would do it for you. She didn't know why the plane had circled the island or if in fact it had done. She didn't know if it had indeed been searching for Franc Blakemore, the man who knew the world's secrets. All she knew for sure was that Franc had been on full alert, prepared for the worst and probably very afraid.

She brought her hands up to the sides of his face and touched him tentatively, almost afraid he would break under her touch. His eyes lowered and he looked at her for the first time, and she saw pain there, but no fear.

He made no attempt to kiss her; she had thought that in his relief that the danger was past he would have done. So she would take the initiative, she would show him that she cared because he needed someone and she was here.

She raised her chin and sought his lips, and felt the surprise in the hesitant contact; then she felt the swift surge of heat course through his body. His arms drew her ever harder into him and his lips parted passionately, drawing from the strength she was offering. But then the roles were reversed and she wasn't comforting him any more; he was the comforter, grazing soft, sensual kisses over every inch of her face.

She grasped his head and splayed her fingers in his thick dark hair, caressing and willing him further and further to touch, to devour every last measure of her heated flesh.

He moved her slightly away from him and she tensed, fearing rejection; but it wasn't rejection he had in mind. Zoe let out a tiny gasp of pleasure and excitement as he tore her thin cotton shirt open at the front. A trickle of moisture ran down between her breasts and his tongue snaked out to capture its sweetness.

Her hands went to his hips, grasping at the coarse fabric of his jeans and drawing him against her. Three years of wanting and fantasising seared any inhibitions from her actions. She was with him all the way, tearing at his clothes as anxiously and as impatiently as he tore at hers; but then his hands stilled.

'I want to look,' he grated throatily. 'I want to see the body that I've dreamed of for so long.'

It seemed the sun was programmed to emerge at that very moment, as if some divine power was responsible for highlighting every seductive contour of her body. The light, warm sunlight slanting in from the narrow windows, dappled her creamy flesh, and the whiteness of the stone walls reflected on his broad frame as he stood in front of her.

He reached forward and loosened her chambray skirt from her waist. It slid to the ground, leaving only her tiny white lace briefs. Her shirt still hung from her shoulders and Franc slid his hands over her breasts but left the shirt intact.

His head dropped forward and his mouth closed over her breast, hungrily drawing her sweetness into his mouth. Every pulse clamoured with need as he drew harder and more passionately on her and then he drew back and let his eyes roam languorously over her once again.

He stepped back and started to remove his clothes; his jeans fell to the floor, and Zoe watched in wonderment, her desire so desperately close to the surface that it was in danger of exploding.

'Are you disappointed?' she murmured as he made no attempt to touch but just stood watching her engorged breasts rise and fall.

'Disappointed in perfection?' He smiled and his eyes were bright with desire. 'It's not possible. And you, Zoe, my perfect one—are you disappointed?'

He was so beautiful, naked before her, so immense and powerful and sexual. Her body ached for him, for the contact of flesh on flesh, for the insistence of his arousal against her hips, her groin, her thighs and then her secret inner self.

Her tender touch was all the answer she gave him. She reached out and caressed his arousal, smoothed both hands over its silken tautness. He let out a gravelled moan of submission and came towards her, grasping her hips, his thumbs caressing under the lace, teasing her and grinding her back against the wall. Zoe's back arched against the cool stone wall behind her as he eased the briefs from her bottom, drawing them down till she was free for him. With an impassioned intake of breath Zoe

cried out as she felt the so longed for pressure between her thighs.

Franc's strong, powerful hands lifted her hips and
in the same moment he entered her, impaling her
against his hard flesh, grasping her on to him in a
union so forceful, so complete, so compulsive that
they both moaned out loud.

Zoe clung to him as he supported her, drawing
her legs around him as she had done once before.
His movements were rapid, his kisses delivered with
an urgency she matched, and then Franc let out a
deep moan.

'Sweet lord, not like this,' he hoarsed roughly.
He withdrew from her and she clung to him to keep
her balance, slightly bemused and flushed with
desire. He lifted her chin and kissed her heavy
eyelids and gathered her strongly against his raging
body. 'I promised myself when I made love to you
again it would be like the first time—tender and
erotic, touching and stimulating—not like this,
against some unyielding wall. I want to taste you,
drink in your desire, for you to taste me. I want it
to go on forever. I want to be inside you forever.'

Zoe clung to him as he lifted her and carried her
to the raised dias in the sitting-room and set her
among the deep, downy Turkish cushions. The rain
had perfumed the earth and the citrus trees outside,
and their brief, frantic coupling in the kitchen had
perfumed their bodies with the scent of love. Zoe
lay beneath him, gazing up into his beautiful face
as he caressed her body, smoothing his hands so
sensuously over her fiery skin till she writhed under
the sweet torture of the tantalising pleasure.

The three years without him hadn't existed. There had been no life between that night in Switzerland and this balmy, storm-abated afternoon. There was no future either, just now and Franc and his love and him touching her and kissing her and her returning each and every one of his pleasures till finally and in sheer desperation he entered her for that final plunge into hedonism.

Their furious climax, their simultaneous burst of molten fire, their gritted cries of pulsing release and the throbbing aftermath as their raging heated bodies sank into exhausted languidness was as predictable and as certain as the sun rising and setting every day for eternity.

CHAPTER SIX

ZOE lay next to him that night, in his bed, with the bedside cabinet next to them a hideous reminder of the fragility of his life.

'What's wrong?' Franc murmured next to her. He gathered her into his arms, and she let him because to protest would be wrong now.

She should have protested before he had loved her on the Turkish cushions; but now it was too late. By allowing him to love her she had made some sort of commitment. He had taken it for granted she would sleep with him from now on.

'I can't sleep,' she murmured back.

He laughed softly and ran a hand over her still swollen breasts. 'What a little paradox you are. You're supposed to fall into a delicious sleep after——'

'After sex?' she finished for him.

'Stop that,' he ordered lightly.

Zoe stroked her thumb across his jawline. He was right, of course. 'I'm sorry,' she whispered. And she was. She supposed all women felt like this when they were in love—so very unsure of themselves. But this was more than just uncertainty about how he felt for her. They weren't just on this island to wind up his company; there was more. She wanted to know about the plane and why he had been so afraid and kept them both inside as it had circled, but fear of his answer kept the question buttoned

106

inside her. She couldn't bear to think that he was
in any sort of danger.

'Sleep, darling,' he husked, and kissed her brow
tenderly.

Zoe relaxed. No, she didn't want to think any
more and she wouldn't. She was with the man she
loved and it had to be enough.

Some time in the night she awoke. She thought
she heard a voice, and reached for Franc, but he
wasn't there. She couldn't have heard voices, she
thought sleepily; they were the only two people in
the world. Then suddenly he was there, warm and
solid next to her, and reaching out for her.

'What the hell are you doing in here?'

Zoe spun round, her eyes brimming with tears at
her discovery. 'You . . . you left the door open.'

She had thought he was at the store house on the
beach—and was so shocked when she had opened
the door of the spare bedroom that she hadn't heard
him come back.

'I did nothing of the sort!' Franc stormed,
crossing the room and grasping her wrist to pull her
out of the room—the room that had been locked
against her.

'OK!' Zoe cried, pulling back from him and
holding her ground. 'You didn't leave the door
open—you're too damned efficient for that. I . . . I
found the key——'

'Found? You can't find something that wasn't
lost!'

'The key fell out of your jeans pocket when you
were taking a shower,' Zoe told him hotly.

'Keys don't fall out of jeans——'

'For God's sake! I went to hang up your jeans and the key fell out! What does it matter anyway?' she stormed at him. No tears now, just blind fury that he was being so picky about something so damned serious. 'You have no reason to carry a key with you on this island—unless of course it was to prevent me getting into this room, which I now see to be the case. What happened to the open-doors-at-all-times theory?'

'This has nothing to do with you. Why the hell did you come in here?' he blazed, fists clenched at his side, his eyes so dark and glittery with anger.

He was furious with her, and Zoe didn't understand why. She was the one who should be furious. He hadn't been honest with her, but now he would have to be.

'It's I who should be asking the questions,' she retorted. She flung her hand out towards the two-way radio on the table by the window. 'I've woken up these past few nights, thought I was dreaming and hearing voices. But I wasn't dreaming, was I? You were talking on that radio, weren't you? Don't deny it, just don't you dare deny it.'

There was a pause before he answered, and why did Zoe imagine he was debating what to tell her? Oh, God, what had happened? The last few days had been heaven. They had loved and laughed and loved again and again, and now this. But her own stupid fault. She shouldn't have pried but, if she hadn't . . .

'I've no intention of denying it,' he told her quietly. 'I talk on the radio every night; there is nothing sinister about that.'

Sinister. Zoe rolled the word around her head. It was a word she hadn't thought of. Mysterious, yes, not sinister. That old apprehension was there again.

'Why didn't you tell me? Why keep the door locked when you were forever urging me to keep mine open?

'It has nothing to do with you,' Franc repeated levelly. 'I have to keep in contact with certain people——'

'What certain people?'

Franc's eyes narrowed. 'Don't push me, Zoe; I don't like being pushed.'

'In other words, mind my own business?'

He took her arm quite firmly this time and half pulled her out of the room, slamming the door shut behind them. 'Key,' he demanded outside in the hall. Zoe gave it to him; it was hot where it had been clasped tightly in her hand after unlocking the room and making her nerve-racking discovery.

'Franc,' she implored—temper wasn't getting her anywhere with him—'you are hiding something from me and I want to know what. You owe me an explanation.'

He walked away from her. Not a word passed his lips. Zoe spurred after him and caught him in the kitchen as he was about to power out of the kitchen door to the terrace and heaven knew where after that.

'Why won't you tell me the truth?' she screamed and then her shoulders sagged and her voice came less hysterically. She would have to drag her fears into the open, the fears she had buried since her first suspicions. 'I know! Look, I know what the problem is——'

'You know nothing, Zoe!' He spun to face her. His voice was almost contemptuous. 'You know nothing about anything.'

Zoe clutched her arms about her, more hurt than she had ever been in her life.

'Meaning I'm some sort of empty-headed bimbo?' She laughed then. 'But of course that is exactly what I am, and why you brought me here. Three years ago you took me for exactly the same reason and here is history repeating itself. And I've fallen for it yet again. Yes, I'm a bimbo—fancy me forgetting that!'

She tore past him, out of the house and off down through the citrus grove.

'And where the devil do you think you are running to?' he called after her. 'Nowhere to run to, Zoe!'

'Huh! That's what you think. I'm going to swipe down a few trees and whittle myself a boat and get the hell off this island!'

He joined her later on the beach where she was sprawled sulkily on the sand, piling small shells into a heap.

'I thought you would at least have had the hull finished by now.'

'It isn't funny,' she uttered miserably.

Franc sighed as he crumbled down to the sand next to her, stretching out his long bare brown legs and running his toes down her shin—a gesture that had Zoe's heart reaching out for him, wanting it all to be normal and right; but it wasn't. His life was so strange and different and scary.

'No, it isn't funny at all,' he agreed. 'Nor is prying into my private affairs.'

'But you've drawn me into your private affairs. By bringing me here you've involved me in your life,' Zoe insisted.

'I brought you here to work——'

'In and out of your bed!'

'Don't talk like that.'

'Why? Because you don't like hearing the truth? Because it isn't very ladylike for a woman to say what a man thinks?'

'This man doesn't think that way.'

Zoe snorted and knocked over the pile of shells and immediately started building them up again. 'This man could have fooled me.'

'I brought you here to help me with my work——'

'And help you out in bed!'

It was he who scattered the shells this time, angrily. 'Will you quit that talk? What we are doing in bed is for us both, and for heaven's sake stop calling it ''bed''. We make love, Zoe, both of us. Don't make it sound as if you're an unwilling partner.'

Zoe lay back in the sand and closed her eyes to the glare of the sun and sky. She would have liked to shut out the glare of her love for Franc from her heart too, but some things were impossible. Oh, it had been so good. Long, languorous days of sweet, sweet pleasure and love and desire. Swimming, making love on the beach, fishing, making love in the sea, making love whenever the desire took them. Now it had soured so badly that there was no going back.

'Willing partner? You make it sound like a business deal,' she murmured miserably.

'It isn't that; you know it isn't that.'

So what is it? she wanted to ask, but the fear of the truth drove the words back down her throat. She sat up then and gazed pleadingly at him. 'I don't know anything about a man who carries a gun, locks a radio away from the woman sharing his life; at this moment . . .' she drew breath '. . . all I know is that you are in . . . in some sort of danger, and if you think keeping it from me will help it go away, it won't.'

'This is my problem,' he told her solemnly. He sat gazing out to sea, his arms clasped around his knees.

'Yet you think nothing of involving me in *your* problem.' Her heart began to pulse at what she had just uttered. Her insides went cold and she wondered why she hadn't seen it all before. It had been one of those unwelcome thoughts she had buttoned away out of sight, too afraid to think them.

'You aren't involved,' Franc told her, but Zoe didn't hear.

Shakily she got to her feet as if suddenly she was weighted with lead. She had been incredibly stupid and blind.

'You bastard!' she breathed heatedly. 'I . . . I see it all now.' Her breath would hardly come, so deep was the hurt. 'You're using me, some . . . some sort of . . . cover——'

'What the blazes do you think you are talking about?' he growled, leaping to his feet and grasping her shoulders.

She shrank away from him, her eyes bright and wide and terribly hurt.

'You brought me here, you're ... keeping me here ...' She swallowed hard. 'You're in danger; someone is after you and you're hiding, and you've brought me here to fool everyone into thinking you are just here to work——'

'Stop this, Zoe,' Franc warned. 'Stop this crazy reasoning.'

'It isn't crazy!' she sobbed. 'I know now. I understand everything. Not using Theo's yacht ... the two taxis in Athens ... rapid clearance at the airport ... the parachute jump ...' Her head was spinning as it all jumbled in front of her eyes ... the apprehension she had felt—she had *known* something wasn't quite right. 'You were covering your tracks ... You ... you even drugged me...to keep me...to keep me quiet...so I wouldn't ask questions ... wouldn't make a fuss ...'

Franc suddenly released her as if she were contaminated. His hands dropped to his sides and he just stood watching the distress in her face and making no offer to soothe it away. She inwardly prayed he would grind out a denial, but her prayers weren't to be considered today.

'It's true, then?' she husked bitterly when he offered no heated denial. 'I'm just some sort of decoy. You'd be easy to find on your own, but with me in tow you look just like any number of holiday-makers frequenting these islands.' Even honeymooners, she thought desperately, two lovers in a sensuous world of their own. Oh, God, how cruelly she had been used.

'And all your work...that...that was just a ploy
to get me here. You're not winding up your
company. It was all lies...to make me believe...'
Oh, please deny something, anything, she added
silently.

She watched his eyes, studied them intently for
some sign. They were as smoky as wood fire and
equally inscrutable. She wanted to run, but how
many times had he said it was useless to try? She
had nowhere to go, and running didn't solve
anything.

'I want to know, Franc,' she cried bitterly. 'I want
to hear it from your own lips—why you did such
a cruel and selfish thing by bringing me here, exposing me to the same danger you're running from.
If you're a target, so am I; so why?'

No denial, no words of comfort, false or
otherwise. She had nothing to fight with if he didn't
fight back and fuel the battle. But what battle? In
his eyes there wasn't one; in his eyes she was something to while away the days with till the danger
was over.

She held his expressionless eyes for a fleeting
second and then moved away from him, along the
beach, far away from him, but never far enough.
The end of the world wouldn't be far enough away
from him.

'Finished sulking?'

He held a mug of coffee out to her as she lay
coiled on the Turkish cushions. She refused it with
a shake of her head and lowered her eyes back down
to the paperback she had clasped tightly in her
hand. A warm breeze drifted in from the window,

swaying the oil lamp to and fro above her head. Cicadas throbbed outside in the citrus trees and the rush of sea over the reef was the only other sound.

'You've had no food tonight; at least take the coffee I made for you.'

She looked up at him then, contemptuously. 'Not another morsel will pass my lips till I'm off this island, Franc Blakemore,' she told him acidly.

'Hunger strike?'

'Yes,' she returned blatantly. 'I refuse to eat till you get on that radio and summon my freedom.'

'You will starve before that happens,' he told her levelly.

There wasn't even hurt any more. 'And I will die if I stay here with you. I'll be shot or garrotted or tortured to death by some gruesome terrorist faction out for your blood, not mine. People like that don't recognise innocence or even women.'

'Don't be so hysterical, Zoe; this is life, not the movies.'

'Yes, my life, not yours to play Russian roulette with.'

'I'm not playing with your life, I'm...' He suddenly let out a hopeless sigh and turned away.

'You're *what*?' She didn't want him to keep walking away like this. Couldn't he give her some answers? Though for what reason? She knew what she knew, and hated him for it.

'I can't give you an explanation——'

'Top secret, is it?' she goaded, slamming shut the book and tossing it down on a nearby cushion.

He turned and looked at her. 'Sometimes ignorance is bliss, Zoe, and before you hit back with your hurt feelings just stop and think for a minute.

I could have picked any woman off the street of any major city and brought her here to do what you have accused me of doing, but I didn't.'

'No, you picked me!' Zoe fought back. 'For some strange reason that eludes me. Oh, I forgot.' Her voice switched to scathing sarcasm. 'I'm the best, aren't I? If you bite the dust you might as well bite the dust with the best.'

'No one is going to die, Zoe.' He said it so calmly, so lethally that it frightened her more than if he had said they *were* going to die.

'So why the gun? Why the fear when that plane came over?'

She thought this was another question he was going to walk away from, but he held his ground and gazed at her. She imagined pain in his eyes, but the light was bad and the likes of him had no emotions anyway.

'If I showed any fear it wasn't for myself, I assure you.'

Zoe raised her dark brows. 'So you were afraid for me. Is that supposed to mean you care?' She gave him no chance to answer. 'What a paradox *you* are. You expose me to danger by bringing me here and then get uptight when my life is threatened. Sorry, I don't believe that; you were shivering for your own skin, not mine.'

He tensed at that and she regretted saying it. Whatever the reasons for him bringing her here didn't alter the fact that he was in danger. She looked away from him, not able to bear the look in his eyes. Damn him, he made her feel guilty for only thinking of herself. It was him they were after, and what was her life without his?

'I'm going to bed,' she breathed, and uncoiled herself from the cushions.

'My bed or your own?'

'Need you ask?'

'If I was sure I wouldn't, but I'm never sure of anything with you, Zoe.'

Her head jerked towards him at that. He held her eyes for a fleeting second and then he looked away as if he couldn't bear the refusal she was obviously going to utter.

'My bed. Nothing stays the same forever.' She echoed his words as she walked to the door.

'Leave your door open, Zoe, because nothing has changed either.'

She did leave her bedroom door open, safe in the knowledge that he wouldn't take advantage of it, for now she knew and understood the reasons for the request. If someone did manage to get on this island and into the villa, open doors were safer.

She lay in bed, sleepless and restless, tossing those thoughts around in her head. She didn't want him to die or suffer, but she felt used, the love he didn't know about abused. She ached with fear and love and sorrow. She would have willingly made the choice to be with him in his hour of need, if he had asked. But he hadn't asked, just taken and used and abused. He needed someone, and had picked her because she had been such a pushover three years ago.

Zoe buried her face in her pillow and cried into the night.

*　　*　　*

'Are you serious about this hunger strike?' he asked at breakfast. He looked washed out, as if he'd been up all night.

Zoe sat at the kitchen table sipping water and fighting every urge in her body not to jump up and wrap her arms around him. She wanted to comfort him, and needed comfort herself.

'I told you, I'm not eating till you summon a boat or a helicopter or a space shuttle to get us off this island.'

'Us, not just yourself?'

She'd made a decision last night before slipping into a fitful sleep. She loved him, foolish though it was, and she wanted them both off this island, not just herself. But once off she never wanted to see him again. He could go back to his mistresses and his embassies and she would go back to her life with Theo... Oh, God, the thought appalled her.

'Both of us would be safer somewhere else,' she stated firmly. 'We landed by parachute; so could some crazed terrorist determined enough.'

'I'm touched by your concern for my safety— wish that I could have been touched by yourself in my bed. It was a long night without you.'

He still had the power to flame embarrassment to her cheeks. 'How can you think of such a thing when your life is in the balance?'

'Men think of sex constantly; didn't you know that?'

It struck her that the skilful switch of subject was a cover-up for his anxiety, but she was too hurt to dwell on it. 'No,' she sighed, 'but it doesn't surprise me.' Sex—he'd said it, and it wasn't a figure

of speech. She was sex to him, not love or even
mundane desire, just sex, pure and simple.

'Who is after you, then? Some mistress's irate
husband?'

'I don't take other men's property.'

Zoe shrugged. 'What a sexist remark. A wife is
a husband's *property*, is she?'

Franc sighed heavily. 'What do you want, Zoe?
A full-blooded debate on man's domination of
woman? Well, you aren't going to get it from me.'

'No, you just practise it!' Zoe spat back. 'You're
no different from Theo, keeping my mother a
prisoner to punish her for the wrong she did him
years ago, and you're no different from the father
I've never known. He took his pleasure and refused
to face the consequences. Men are all take and no
give.'

Franc's face darkened and she thought she had
hit a few right notes there. How they all hated being
crossed.

'Has it ever occurred to you that your father
could have had good reason not to acknowledge
you?'

Zoe swivelled to watch him putting the coffee-
pot on the gas.

'It occurred to me that he was married, yes,' she
murmured, feeling a strange unease that he should
bring that up and know so much about a subject
that was nothing to do with him. The unease
doubled as she recalled Theo's remark about Franc
looking no further. 'I suppose this is leading up to
you telling me you're married too.' Zoe honestly
didn't know how she had got that out. The need

to know had outweighed the pain his answer might give her.

He turned to look at her and his face was darkly serious. 'No, I'm not married, but would it have made any difference to you? I don't recall you asking such a question before.'

Zoe gulped at her water. That was so painfully true. It had never crossed her mind that the stranger she had made love with could have been another woman's husband. But no, the rumours—the mistresses, no rumours of a wife. But then she hadn't heard those rumours before she had given her heart. She understood suddenly—understood how her mother had fallen so easily and had gone on hoping for so long.

'Neither of us asked any questions that night,' she murmured.

She heard him moving behind her, pouring coffee, and then he was sitting across from her, handsome and beautiful, tearing at her heart.

'Not that night or now,' he told her solidly.

Zoe shook her head. 'And you won't give me any answers anyway.'

'I've just admitted I'm not married.'

'That isn't important——'

'I'd say it was very important in this relationship.'

'We're not having a relationship,' she told him sharply. 'I didn't mean that it was of no concern to me if you had a wife somewhere, I meant that you are not honest with me in other ways. You won't tell me who is threatening you or why.'

'Because it won't make any difference to the situation; it won't make it all go away.'

'So someone *is* out for your blood?' Her eyes were wide and appealing to him for the truth, but falling on stony ground with him. 'OK,' she sighed after a very meaningful silence. 'You don't want to trust me. I'm not fit to be confided in. I'm just the bit of light relief you brought along to ease your tension when the going got tough.' She stood up and was about to leave but he grasped her wrist and forced her back down into her seat.

His grip was fierce and his eyes equally fierce. 'I care enough about you not to burden you; isn't that enough for you? Can't you accept that?'

Zoe tightened her lips and wrestled her wrist from his hand. 'If you cared enough about me you wouldn't have brought me here in the first place. You are on the run, not me. I dread to think what horrible lies you told Theo to get him to agree to this.'

'I don't lie!' he breathed emphatically.

'You skirt the truth, though, so it all means the same.'

Slowly he stood up, not taking his eyes from her. 'Sometimes in life skirting the truth is a safe option, preferable to facing an unwelcome fact——'

'You must have skirted the truth to Theo, because if he had known the real reason why you brought me here he would never have agreed to it. So you are a coward as well as a deceiver,' she taunted.

Franc's face tightened and she wished she hadn't said that. He was many things, but not a coward.

'I'm sorry,' she murmured, lowering her eyes. 'You're not a——'

'Maybe you're right for once, Zoe,' he said quietly. 'I may well be a coward, because if I damned well weren't I *wouldn't* have brought you here.'

Her head jerked up and her eyes widened. 'And what do you mean by that?'

He raked a hand through his hair. 'Nothing, forget it.' He lowered his hand to his side and Zoe noted how it clenched into a fist immediately. Strange, but that troubled her more deeply than anything else. 'And forget this idiotic hunger strike of yours, Zoe. We're staying on this island till I see fit to leave it. I want to walk away from here with you at my side, upright, not laid out on a stretcher.

A tremor of sudden fear racked through Zoe. It could be him on the stretcher, not her. She bit her lip. Why was she giving him such a hard time when his life was in the balance? She loved him, didn't she? She should be making life easier for him, but why, when he had exposed her to such danger? If he had any true feelings for her he wouldn't have done that. The thought that he didn't care, in spite of his statement that he did, spurred her next words.

'Me on a stretcher wouldn't be good for your skin when Theo sees me,' she murmured.

He laughed then, almost in relief, Zoe thought. 'Theo isn't a consideration, Zoe; I just don't like my women skin and bone.'

'Well, there's an incentive for instant anorexia.'

'That's my girl,' Franc breezed, considerably less tense. 'I'd much rather you spent your time backbiting me than trying to probe my motivations for bringing you here.'

'I don't need to probe; I know. But by the time we do leave here you'll wonder why you bothered.'

'That won't be anything new. The thought has crossed my mind several times already.'

That hurt, and as usual her hurt fired her defence. 'Getting bored with me already?' She shrugged. 'Can't say it comes as a surprise; you've battled your sexual way through every embassy in the world. Women must be as common as continental breakfasts in your life.'

He placed a hand on the table and leaned over her. 'And the continental breakfasts far more satisfying in most cases. Now, are you going to eat any breakfast or am I going to force-feed you?'

'Well, you've force-fed me everything from sedatives to lies, so I'll pass on that, thank you, and make myself something to eat.'

'Good girl,' he said with a grin, and turned and sauntered out of the door to the terrace.

Zoe sat where she was, in no rush to make herself something to eat. She watched through the open doorway as he strolled across the citrus grove to the beach, his hands plunged deep in his shorts pockets. There was something about the set of his shoulders that pulled desperately at her heart. A brave face— that was what he was putting on. Maybe for her benefit . . . of course for her benefit; there was no one else to put on a face for.

Oh, God, she loved him. Not for that but just for being Franc Blakemore. Slowly she stood up and went to the door, straining her eyes to see him through the trees. His reasons for bringing her here were irrelevant. He'd brought her and no one else, and he had made love to her here, and you couldn't fake the feelings they had for each other when they were making love. Suddenly she wanted to go to him, to hold him and tell him she wanted him to be safe. So what was stopping her? Pride, hurt, fear—yes, all of that. She went to turn away from the door but it was then that something caught her eye.

Zoe stepped out on to the terrace. There was a patch through the branches of the citrus trees where you could clearly see a large expanse of sea. There was a boat moored out there!

Hesitant at first, she stood watching it, the fear creeping up her spine and chilling her bones, then she started to run, her heart screaming out her fear, spurring her on and on. She stumbled, righted herself, gathered her thin cotton skirt into her clenched fists and scrambled on and on along the stony pathway.

'Franc!' she cried as she slithered to a halt in the sand.

He was standing by the water's edge, kicking his feet in the gentle surf. He hadn't seen the boat! He hadn't heard her warning cry.

'Franc!' she screamed again and hurled herself across the sand to him.

He turned and looked across at her blundering towards him, startled by her cry. She flung herself at him, hammering into his body, overbalancing him as he reached out for her. They both fell into the water and as the warm sea shushed and covered her face it brought with it a warm blackness that whipped her last cry of fear from her lips.

CHAPTER SEVEN

THE darkness receded and Franc was there, hovering over her, his wonderful face showing such deep concern that it must mean...

'Are you OK?' he breathed, crouching over her.

She nodded and struggled to a sitting position on the beach. She was soaking wet and so was he. The surf frothed at his feet. She remembered...the boat...and her heart fired fear through her veins.

'Franc, the boat! I saw it!' she cried, trying to look past him.

He stood up, reached down for her hands and hauled her to her feet.

'It's gone,' he told her gently.

Relief swamped her but she took a precautionary glance over his shoulder nevertheless.

'It's all right,' he reassured her, 'it was one of mine.'

Her mouth dropped open and then snapped shut abruptly. 'Yours? What do you mean, yours? I thought you didn't own anything.' He was still holding her hands and she tried to free herself, but he wouldn't allow it.

'When I said it was one of mine I didn't mean it literally. They were my men on the boat.'

'Your men? What do you mean, your men?'

'Will you stop asking such banal questions, Zoe?' He let go of her hands and shifted them to her shoulders. 'I have security men too and they were just checking that all was well here.'

He was smiling at her and she saw nothing amusing in that statement. It simply meant he must be in even more danger than she had thought. Her eyes darkened fretfully and her shoulders stiffened under his touch. The touch turned to a soothing caress and she felt the tension ease.

'You should have told me,' she said softly, lowering her head. 'I . . . I panicked.'

'I'm glad you did.'

Her head shot up. 'Glad, are you?' she flamed. 'Yes, I suppose you must be. That's how you get your pleasure, terrifying the wits out of poor defenceless females . . .'

He started to laugh then.

'It isn't funny!' she wailed, trying to wriggle out of his clutches.

'But it is,' he insisted. 'You're not a poor defenceless female, sweet one; you are a very brave lady, rushing to the defence of the man you love——'

'Oh, no, you don't!' she screamed, and this time she was free of him, stepping back and tensing herself in defence of her emotions. She had made yet another mistake in her life, rushing to him like that . . . showing she cared. Oh, she hated him for exposing her love, but she could get out of it, quite easily. 'I was . . . I was thinking of myself . . . If anything . . . if anything happened to you . . .'

He was still grinning. 'You would be alone here?'

'Yes,' she breathed hotly. 'And . . . and I don't know how to operate the radio. I wouldn't know what to do . . .'

'Perhaps I'd better show you, then, and perhaps I'd better show you where the first-aid kit is in case you have to remove any bullets from my back——'

She let out a strangled cry then and felt dizzy again as the beach, the sea and the sky merged into a haze of blue and white. She flung her arms around his neck and clung to him, sobbing into the crook of his shoulder.

'Now do you still want to deny you care for me?' he husked, wrapping his arms tightly around her.

'You bastard,' she croaked, trying to stop the tears, her chest shuddering with the effort.

His hand smoothed her wet hair. 'Yes, I am,' he agreed, and there was no humour or laughter in his tone. He wasn't teasing her or mocking her. 'But if you won't tell me exactly how you feel I have to use trickery to find out.'

'And... and why... why do you need to know?' She was tempting him now, quietly urging him to make the same commitment she had—that she cared for him and his life because without his life there was none for her.

He eased her away from his shoulder to look down on her tear-streaked face.

'Because I was beginning to think you were only concerned for your own skin.'

Her eyes widened painfully to huge liquid brown orbs that must surely reflect the disappointment of that remark. She had expected more, so much more.

Her heart strengthened and so did her resolve not to be hurt any more. 'As one human being to another I wouldn't want anything to happen to you,' she told him bravely. 'I would show the same concern to anyone.'

'Oh, dear,' he uttered gravely though she sensed it was forced, 'there was I thinking the concern was solely for Franc Blakemore.'

'Don't flatter yourself.' She turned away from him then and started to make her way back to the villa, retracing steps she had just made, but with a different power behind them. She had rushed to him with love and fear in her heart; they were still there, but interwoven with a dragging hopelessness. She had given him such opportunities there to make it all right, but he had skirted them as skilfully as he skirted any truth in his life.

She left him on the beach, not glancing back, not wanting to accentuate her hurt.

'So what exactly are we waiting for?' she asked later at dinner.

He sat across from her, forking his pasta with indifference. He had cooked the supper with her as back-up, clearing the utensils as he had worked. The result was acceptable but hardly taste-bud-tiltillating.

'What do you mean?' he asked.

'I mean is this crazed killer expected to pounce——?'

'Who said it was a killer?'

Zoe raised her dark brows at that. 'Ah, perhaps not a killer, then, but a kidnapper. Interesting thought. I wonder how much your ransom would be and if there was anyone out there willing to cough up and save your life?'

He smiled. 'Would you?'

'Pay up to save you? What are you worth?'

'To someone who cared enough for me, a king's ransom.'

'I don't have a king's ransom. In spite of my lifestyle with Theo I have nothing of my own.'

'No piggy bank?'

'Not even that.'

'You'd have to pay with your body, then,' he said.

'It's worthless.'

His eyes were intense as they bridged the table to meet hers. 'To me it's priceless,' he told her softly.

The words caressed her heart and nervously she ran her tongue over her lips, wishing that her heart and not her body was priceless to him. She was the first to break the eye contact.

'So... are you in danger of being kidnapped?' She'd prefer that to a terrorist out for his life.

'It's always a possibility. There are any number of factions out there who'd find it advantageous to take me as a hostage.'

Zoe pushed her plate away and leaned her arms on the table. It still wasn't a straight answer to her question but she had learned by now that Franc Blakemore was an expert at avoiding issues. But maybe in his way he was protecting her—the least she knew, the better, from a security point of view. But she wished he would confide in her, just to prove that he trusted her.

'Is that why you're such a free spirit? Not wanting to settle, not wanting to own anything?' she asked.

'It's why I'm giving it up now. I don't want to go on living such an insular life.' He stood up and cleared the plates from the table, and Zoe watched him.

'So you *are* giving it all up. I thought all this mundane paperwork was just for my benefit, a ploy to get me here, a cover-up for the real reason you're here, in hiding.'

'A ploy it wasn't, mundane it was, but none the less necessary. I'm getting out to pursue the lighter things of life. You can't live in the hot seat forever. I'm getting too old for all this cloak-and-dagger routine.' He poured their coffees, brought them back to the table and sat down.

'And how old are you, Grandad?'

'Thirty-three going on seventy-eight.'

Zoe laughed. 'Poor soul, I feel sorry for you.'

'Sorry enough to give an old man some comfort and warmth tonight?' His voice was very meaningful but with a hint of humour which dispelled her anxiety at his veiled suggestion.

Her eyes twinkled. 'I'm sure I can rustle up some cocoa and a security blanket for you.'

'I was thinking more of scented skin and the security of your legs wrapped around mine.' His hand reached out and his fingers traced small circles on her arm.

His touch was fire on her skin, temptation to her senses. Just one small touch and the need erupted, surging love and yet hopelessness to her heart. She needed him and he obviously needed her, and nothing had really changed since last they had loved.

She moved her fingers over his, a tiny gesture that spoke volumes from her soul. An acceptance as inevitable as the request. The door was always open.

The night was insufferably hot and their love-making somehow different. There was fire and urgency but an underlying desperation that Zoe didn't quite understand. It was with her, in her heart, and she understood that, but his urgency she didn't understand, and could only suppose it was his worry perhaps culminating in the force of his ardour.

When he entered her, after flaming her desire to the point of suffering, it was with a groan of despair, a heated cry that had her pressing her lips urgently against his pulsing throat. She wanted to cry that she loved him and always had and always would; she wanted him to know that she would always be there for him, but no words would come to her lips. They lay muted in her throat as his thrusts grew ever more powerful, whirling her into that secret world of hedonism he had created for her. When at last they couldn't hold back, grasping at each other in that mysterious euphoria as liquid fire pulsed crazily between them, she murmured just one word, his name, plaintively cried out in the heat of the night.

He could do nothing to hold back the fire that pulsed into her; he swelled and exploded inside her, but she sensed the release wasn't complete, as if he had more to give and wanted more in return, and she didn't understand what or why.

They lay hot and wet in each other's arms and the usual tranquillity following the tempest of

emotions didn't come. She knew he was still awake,
his breathing not deep and relaxed but shallow and
disturbed as if...as if she hadn't pleased and satisfied him.

She turned her face to him and still the words
wouldn't come; the soft murmur of what her heart
wanted to say was still elusive. She mouthed kisses
against his neck, stroked her hands over his body,
wanting him to make love to her again in the hope
it would release the words she couldn't speak. Her
fingers trailed down to caress him, slicked over his
tautness. He was still aroused, and that disturbed
her. She hadn't pleased him, she hadn't satisfied
him...

He stilled her hand, clasped his own over hers,
and turned his head to claim her mouth in an impassioned kiss as if he too couldn't put into words
what he felt. They fell asleep in the hot night air,
neither having spoken a word.

Zoe woke later in the night and Franc wasn't with
her. Her hand slid out and smoothed over the sheet
where he should have been. She strained her ears
and heard the murmur of his voice. Just a murmur,
though, nothing more. She rolled on to her back
and wondered who those certain people were whom
he spoke to every night. His men, reporting on the
whereabouts of the hostage-seekers? Zoe twisted
her head and buried her face in the pillow. Franc
Blakemore gave nothing, not his heart or his trust.
She knew as much about him as she had known
that night in Switzerland—nothing.

Zoe awoke alone and instinctively knew she had
been alone most of the night. She got up and slid

a T-shirt over her head and climbed into the shorts
she had discarded the night before. She went to the
bathroom and showered and washed her hair, wondering what Franc was doing.

Franc! Fear charged her again and, wrapping a
towel round her, she dashed to the kitchen.

He was sitting at the table, his head in his hands,
and though she was relieved to see he was safe the
fear didn't pass. He looked terrible. Unshaven, hair
tousled, his chest somehow caved in as if having
suffered a crippling blow that had winded him.

'Franc?' she murmured with a worried frown
marring the usual clearness of her forehead.
Barefoot, she stepped across the tiles to him.

His head jerked up as if she had startled him.
His hand raked through his hair and he made an
effort to get himself together. He stood up and
forced a smile.

'We're leaving. The boat to pick us up will be
here in an hour.' His tone was clipped and formal
in spite of the smile.

'I don't understand.' Her dark eyes were wide
with surprise. 'What's happened?'

He didn't answer for a minute but turned to light
the gas under the coffee. She had the distinct impression he didn't want to look her straight in the
face. She remembered last night's lovemaking. He
had given but not given, had somehow held back
from her in a way she hadn't understood. He had
grown tired of her, was bored, was ready to move
on to the next woman. Oh, God, what sort of
woman was she for thinking that way? He had been
in grave danger here and now it seemed the danger

was over and this was how it affected him—and it had nothing to do with sex.

'The radio last night . . . you've heard something. The danger, is it over? Have your men found the . . . the people who were after you?'

He turned and looked at her then; his gray eyes were dull and vacant, not relieved as she might have expected.

He nodded. 'Yes, I heard something. There is no danger, not any more. We are free to go.'

So where was her relief? Of course she was relieved. Franc Blakemore, the man she loved, would live and walk free; but why this despair and confusion inside her? And why wasn't Franc elated as he should be?

She wanted to rush to him and throw her arms around him, but she held back: he held her back by the grim set of his shoulders, by the bleakness that darkened his features.

'Franc,' she uttered softly. 'If . . . if the danger is past and . . . and you are free . . . why . . . why so sad?' Yes, it was a sadness; she saw it now. Not bleakness as she had thought. Her heart thudded. Was he sad because their time together was over?

She went to him then, slid her arms up around his neck. She pressed her face into his shoulder and held him tightly to her heart.

Slowly his arms folded around her and she felt the slow beat of his heart against her ribcage. 'You can tell me all about it now, now it's over,' she murmured.

It was a long time before he answered, a time in which he stroked her head tenderly. His body was taut and strained against hers, and she understood.

The worry couldn't just evaporate away so easily. There had been weeks of tension for him, and it would take time for his old confidence to return. She wanted to give him that confidence.

She raised her head and offered him her lips, and he took them, hesitantly at first and then his body gave a small shudder of submission and the kiss deepened into a fierceness she wasn't sure about. But suddenly he stiffened against her, not in the way she cried out for, but in retreat.

He eased her away from him and she felt the rejection as surely as if he had flooded her burning body with crushed ice. His hands came to her naked shoulders but there was no *frisson* of sensuousness because his touch was cool and off-putting.

'We'd better get our things together; there isn't much time,' he told her levelly.

Her hands dropped to her sides and despair thrust words to her mouth. 'I came with nothing and I'm leaving with nothing,' she told him hoarsely, her eyes stinging with the pain of his cold rejection.

'All the better,' he soothed dully, turning his back on her to attend to the coffee.

She couldn't believe it, the mental slap in the face. Her body shuddered and then she moved, slowly and painfully, to her bedroom.

She was right, she had nothing to pack, and she dressed in what she had come in—the white jeans and the raspberry silk shirt. She dressed slowly, mechanically, only vaguely wondering what would happen to her life now. She was numb with pain. It was over, all over. Franc didn't need her any more.

She tidied her room and stared down at the collection of tiny pink shells gathered on the bedside table, shells she and Franc had gathered together. She scooped them up, held them to her lips for a brief second and then flung them from the window to the citrus grove.

She waited on the beach, kicking her bare feet in the sand, hyping herself up to hate the man who took so much and gave so little in return. She saw the boat on the horizon—no yacht, but a simple fishing boat. It somehow undermined her worth even more.

She felt a hand on her shoulder and flinched away from it. 'Are you all right?' was his question which sealed her heart against him ever more. Couldn't he have said how much he was going to miss her? Perhaps that was to come—but more than likely it wouldn't.

'Why shouldn't I be?' Her agony sharpened sarcasm to her lips. 'Great holiday, great venue, but rotten food and shame about the company.'

'Don't say things like that, Zoe,' he said quietly.

'What did you expect?'

'Nothing, I suppose.'

'Nothing wasn't what you got here, though, Franc Blakemore. I gave everything and you gave nothing. You can't even trust me enough to tell me exactly what has gone on here.'

She knew it was hopeless expecting some sort of relinquishing of his feelings for her—there weren't any. But at the very least, now the pressure was off, he might have told her who he had been running from and why.

'If I thought anything could be gained from telling you, I would.'

The throb of the motor of the fishing boat grew louder.

'I'd like to know, that's all. I'm not looking for any gain. I've shared...' Her voice trailed away. She had shared his life here on this island north of Paradise, south of Utopia, but she hadn't shared his confidence. Actually she had shared his bed and there wasn't much more. She gave herself a mental shake-down. Life would go on. She shrugged. 'So I'm not on loan any more. You can return the borrowed goods to Theo, in not such mint condition as when taken out,' she retorted spitefully, narrowing her aching eyes against the sun and the glare of the sea.

'Is that how you've always seen it—your body on loan?'

'It's how it was and now it's over there's no need to gloss over the truth with any excuses of needing me to help with your work.'

He let out a ragged sigh and said quietly, 'It was never like that. I did need you for my work——'

'And for your leisure and for a cover against the gremlins.' She looked at him then, faced him bravely and stoically. You could only be hurt so much and then a barrier against more hurt grew up for protection. 'Well, the gremlins have gone now and it's all over.'

'But it isn't,' he said reluctantly. 'I'm coming back with you. It isn't completely over yet.'

'Really?' she husked sarcastically. 'Well, I suppose that's something—at least you are escorting me back to my keeper, and of course some terms must be negotiated with Theo. You'll expect some sort of monetary embellishment for my more than secretarial services.'

'Shut up, Zoe,' he grated through his teeth. 'You talk like a whore.'

'And you'd know, of course!'

He said nothing, just watched as the boat came closer, his eyes dark and impenetrable.

Zoe clenched her fists at her side, deflated by his non-existent reply. He wouldn't even give her the satisfaction of a good old row before he left her.

The boat could only come so far and Franc waded out to speak to the two men who had come to pick them up. One of them jumped ashore and went up to the store house, obviously to pick up some of the stuff Franc had packed and didn't want left on the island. Franc came back for her and was about to lift her into his arms to save her getting wet.

'Leave me alone,' she snapped. 'I'm quite capable of getting into that boat on my own.'

It was then that he swung her round to face him, gripping her shoulders so roughly that she winced. There was deep pain in his eyes and she barely had a second to wonder at it before his voice croaked harshly, 'Listen to me, Zoe. It's not going to be easy when we get back, so ease up on the "poor little hurt me"——'

'I'm not hurt!' she stormed back at him, and opened her mouth to tell him the likes of him couldn't hurt her, but hadn't the chance to speak them.

'You are, and I understand, and for the moment I can't do anything about it. I'm hurt myself, by your bitterness and your accusations, and there is so much I want to say, but this isn't the time or the place.'

Her mouth parted but yet again no words came. His touch eased and one hand came to lift a tendril of wind-swept hair from her forehead.

'I'm here for you, Zoe, remember that. I regret what has happened here, the way it happened, and I want to do my best to put it right; but I'm not in a position to do that yet. Once again I must ask you to trust me.'

She stared up at him, the murmur of the sea and the slow throb of the still running engine the only sounds. Was there no end to his cruelty? So he regretted it, but did he have to tell her? Couldn't he have left her with just a whisper of pride?

'Why should I trust you,' she breathed heavily, 'when you've shown no such trust in me? I can't even imagine why the need to trust you after we leave here. I have regrets too, Franc, but I've no intention of trying to put them to rights. I don't care enough to want to do that.'

He must know I'm lying, she thought desperately, and now was the time for him to say it, for him to break her down and force an admission of her love for him—and if she did it would open the way for him. Was she mad? He knew that already. She might have been sedated but she had said it and her body had repeated it often enough. No, he was just grinding her nose in the sand. Well, he didn't know it but he was making it easier for her. Keep up the cold, harsh cruelty and it would metamorphose her love to hate. Easy.

She pulled up the legs of her jeans and waded towards the boat. She clambered in with the help of the other man, who gave her an uncertain smile. She could imagine what was going through his mind, and he'd be right. She sat waiting glumly for Franc.

'No parachutes?' she asked as they came in to land on Theo's private landing strip on his island retreat. They had flown direct from Athens, no need for caution any more. 'And just when I was getting the hang of it,' she quipped.

No response from Franc. She had exhausted her supply of cutting remarks on deaf ears for the whole of the long, exhausting journey home. One good thing about him—he hadn't responded with any more cruelty. She was beginning to regret them now, because she had acted childishly and she had worn him down.

'Franc,' she murmured, as the plane made a small bump on the landing strip and coasted towards the hangar.

'No more, please, Zoe. I've had all I can take.' He looked as if he had too. Pale and gaunt and weary were the only adjectives she could think of to describe him.

'I want to apologise.'

He turned to face her and raised a weary brow. 'And what's the punchline?'

'None,' she murmured. 'I'm just glad to be home and . . . and glad you're safe.'

'That's nice to hear,' he said quietly, and smiled for the very first time in a long while. 'So what is the apology for, and is it spurred by relief that I didn't drug you and fling you out of the plane to get here?'

Ignoring his sarcasm as he had ignored hers for the past hours, she said, 'I've had time to think. I can't forgive you for a lot of things, but you've had a bad time and . . . and I've been childish and rude; I apologise for that.'

'You haven't, as it happens. You have reacted as you should, as I would have expected.'

'Meaning I'm not a very nice person, spoilt and selfish——'

'No, Zoe. I meant that I've put you through hell and back and I deserve your disdain. *I* offer no apologies for that, because the circumstances were beyond my control.'

'I'd think more of you if you admitted to me what the circumstances were.'

There was a long pause before he answered, and in that space of time she watched his face. Remarkable, but she couldn't hate him. Love was strange and not very pleasant. It was full of twists and turns of the rest of your emotions, spinning you ways you didn't want to go. To hell and back was a pretty fair description of what he had put her through.

He sighed and looked at her. 'I can't tell you what you want to hear—life isn't that simple; maybe one day I can and will, but till then you'll have to just live with those regrets of yours.'

'And that's it, is it?' she whispered as he un-buckled his seatbelt and stood up. He said nothing, but leaned down and planted a kiss on the top of her head. She wanted to cry with frustration then, but that old hopelessness washed around her. With tremulous fingers she unbuckled her seatbelt. She was home, and soon Theo would be asking her about her trip, and she would lie and sell her soul to the devil to cover the truth: that she loved a man who used and abused and would probably ask an astronomical sum from him for that pleasure. Perhaps she'd be wiser and get more satisfaction from swinging her anger towards Theo for that, for he was as guilty as Franc.

'There's no one here,' she remarked in the airy reception hall of the villa. 'Theo must be away.' She turned to face Franc and bravely spoke her thanks, desperately trying to play down the despair inside her. 'Thank you for bringing me home. I don't suppose we'll meet again...' Suddenly she felt disorientated, and it wasn't because of the thought that this was the last time she would see him. There was something very wrong here. No Theo, no staff, no buzz of activity.

'I told you it wasn't over yet,' Franc said behind her.

She spun to face him. 'What do you mean?'

'Theo has gone away,' he told her. Such a simple statement but complicated in its implications.

Zoe's eyes narrowed. How come he knew so much? The radio back at the island, perhaps? The thought irritated her intensely.

'Where?' she asked, tight-lipped. Somehow she sensed he would know, and was surprised when he shook his dark head.

'I don't know——'

'You don't know?' she echoed harshly and her eyes went skywards. 'I thought you knew just about everything——'

'Stop it, Zoe,' he ordered, his voice echoing around the marble hall. 'Stop biting at me every second and listen. Theo has gone away for a while and I don't know where. All I know is, he asked me to stay with you——'

'No!' Zoe cried, her pulses skidding. Was there no end to this? She didn't need a keeper. Why couldn't Theo give her some independence? 'I don't need you here,' she went on. She swallowed hard. 'I'm not a child. I'm quite able to look after myself, and frankly I can do with some time on my own.' She raked her hair from her face. She was exhausted from the journey home and she just wanted him to leave so she could have some space to re-evaluate her life. She was going to have to live without Franc Blakemore and somehow get some direction back into her future after he had muddled it so.

'Theo has sent the staff away for a break and there is no one here to look after you.'

'So he asked you to stay with me,' Zoe smirked. 'Well, I don't need you, so you can push off somewhere else.'

'This is where I want to be.' He said it so flatly that she doubted that.

She shrugged. ''Of course, you have nowhere to go; but I'm sure there must be some woman somewhere eager to give you a bed for the night. I'm certainly not going to.' She turned and headed for the curving marble stairs. 'Shut the door after you when you go,' she called out.

She was in her bedroom when he caught up with her. She was just about to fling herself on the bed in a fury of hurt. Theo should have been here. Theo

shouldn't have expected Franc to look after her...
Hell, why? She didn't need anyone!

Franc caught her arm and swung her round to
face him and she saw the look in his eyes. The look
of someone who didn't want to be here. If Theo
had asked him to stay it was certainly not what
Franc Blakemore wanted.

'I'm staying, Zoe. I don't want you to be
alone——'

'I've been alone all my life,' she retorted. 'What
difference now?'

'All the difference in the world.' His grip on her
tightened. 'I'm staying, Zoe. There are no
staff——'

'I don't need staff!'

'You can't live in this huge great place on your
own——'

'Why the sudden concern?' she interrupted in a
fury. She wrenched herself away from his grip. 'My
services have come to an end. You don't need me
and I don't need you any more.' She suddenly
thought of her mother. She wanted to be alone but
it seemed Franc was determined not to let her be;
if she went to her mother's he wouldn't follow. Her
shoulders sagged with weariness. 'I'll go to my
mother's...' She didn't finish, for to her astonishment Franc turned away from her furiously and
pounded a fist against the bedroom door.

A shiver ran through the whole of Zoe's body.
She had seen him mad before, but never, ever like
this. She coiled her arms around herself and with
dry lips waited for him to move. He stood with his
back to her, his head lowered, his fist still bunched
on the door. Then slowly he turned, and that turn

renewed all that old apprehension and fear deep inside her. She knew then that there was something terribly wrong.

'Your mother is away too, Zoe,' he told her, his voice low. 'With Theo. They've gone away, together. For God's sake don't ask me where again because I can't give you an answer, but I'm going to find out, and when I do I'm going to give him a taste of the hell he has put me through these last weeks.'

His bunched fist uncoiled and he brought it up shakily to rake his dishevelled hair from his face. Zoe watched every movement with ice-cold fear in her eyes. Oh, God, what had happened? She dared not ask. Franc had frightened her with his cold threat to Theo for this trauma he was going through.

Slowly his eyes met hers, grey, grey eyes that somehow looked older than time. 'I'm going to make some phone calls now. Why don't you shower and get some rest?'

He said it so intently, so resolutely that the urge to argue died inside her. She nodded, too afraid to argue, too exhausted to question anything he said any more. He closed the door quietly behind him and Zoe was still standing in the middle of the room minutes after he had left.

She was shaken to the roots of her being, afraid and uncertain. Slowly she moved to the bathroom.

CHAPTER EIGHT

ZOE stood out on her balcony, watching Franc pacing round the pool area below. He looked very alone, very preoccupied with his thoughts, which obviously didn't include her otherwise he would have come to her.

The villa had never been so deathly quiet without Theo and the entourage, she'd thought when she had earlier ventured downstairs. Her footsteps had echoed on the cool marble as she'd approached Theo's study, somehow sensing Franc was there. Her instinct was correct; she'd heard him bellowing down the phone.

'I don't care what his instructions are—just find him, for as sure as hellfire I'm not going to tell her!'

There had been more, a fury of words she hadn't heard because her mind had blanked off as if covered by a safety-valve that locked in times of stress. She'd backed away and retreated to the isolation of her bedroom and stayed there, waiting, waiting.

It would be dark soon. The skies flamed with fire and her fingers dug into her palms as she recalled how they had watched the sunset together on the island. Once they had made love on the beach, their naked bodies bathed in fiery light from the rapidly setting sun. They had lain there till the moon had silvered their sated flesh and then they had risen and swum in the darkness, reaching out for each other, touching and caressing as the warm water bathed them.

The memories of that ecstatic time in her life flooded her with new courage. She had to see Franc, if only to find out what was going on.

Her foot was on the bottom step of the stairway when she heard the phone ring. There were phones everywhere, and after two rings it stopped and Zoe presumed Franc had picked it up outside on the patio by the pool. She hurried through the villa to the terrace overlooking the pool, the terrace where Theo had introduced her to the man she had loved for three years. It was all a lifetime ago.

Zoe hung back in the shadows of the columns, straining her ears to hear.

'I did a job, Theo; you have no right to expect more... Yes, I know, but you and Heraklea should have been here... No, damn you! I'm not made of bloody steel... it isn't my place to tell her.'

There was a long, long pause in which Zoe tried desperately to get her swirling thoughts in perspective. Had Theo and her mother gone away to get married and now Theo was expecting Franc to tell her? No, was she crazy? Marriage was a happy event, and Franc wasn't happy about all this at all. And what job? *What* job?

'Don't be such a selfish bastard, Theo. I know Heraklea needs you, but what about Zoe? She isn't a child any more... You're the nearest she's got for as sure as Hades that selfish bitch hasn't given her daughter much love in the past... She's lonely, always has been... Damn you, Koriakis, damn you to hell!' The phone crashed down, coupled with an explosion of exasperation from Franc and then silence.

Zoe wasn't a child any more but Zoe was crying, her body strained back against the cool marble pillars. Bravely she fought the tears, scrubbing at her face with the backs of her hands. Her body was trembling and she didn't know why—she didn't know anything! A small sob escaped into the night and she bit her lip, praying he hadn't heard it.

'Zoe?'

She heard her name called in the darkness and she steeled herself.

'Zoe, are you there?'

She heard a chair scrape on the patio and suddenly she was more afraid than ever. It fired her flight and she ran back into the house, not knowing why when she needed to know so much, but not yet, not yet, because whatever Franc had been ordered to tell her would hurt; she felt it deep inside her.

She was curled on the bed, hugging the pillow, when he finally came to her. She would have locked the door if there had been a lock, would have slid a chest across the door if she had had the strength.

'I've brought you something to eat and drink,' he said softly, placing a tray by the side of the bed.

Zoe uncoiled herself to look at him and then to the tray. 'Brandy?' she uttered weakly, staring at the bottle and the two glasses, scarcely able to focus. Somehow that brandy was ominous.

'Some sandwiches too. You've had nothing to eat today.' He put the plate down on the bedcover and she pushed it away, but accepted the glass of brandy he poured for her.

Franc sat on the edge of the bed, looking tired and gaunt, cupping his brandy in both hands. 'What did you hear?' he asked, not looking at her but staring down at the Persian rug at his feet.

'Nothing and everything, and I don't suppose you will tell me what it all meant anyway. You were rowing with Theo, weren't you?'

He nodded, and she expected more but didn't get it. His restraint angered her and yet somehow gave her strength. She sat up and back against the carved headboard. The brandy warmed her but did little else to take the pain away.

'Are they married?' she whispered.

He gave a cynical laugh. 'Wish it were that simple.'

She noticed his fingers whiten around the goblet and realised this must be painful for him too. He didn't want to be here but Theo had forced it on him.

He spoke at last, slowly and levelly. 'Zoe, Theo loves you and so does your mother——'

'That selfish bitch, you mean?' she interrupted acidly.

'I'm sorry you had to hear that.' He lifted his head and looked at her then. 'I'm sorry you had to hear any of it.'

'So am I,' she murmured. 'I don't know what all this is about but I do know I don't want to hear it from you.' The words came out of their own volition, without pre-thought, but as she realised what she had said she knew it to be true. The phone call had been a mystery but Franc's contribution wasn't. He didn't want to be here, he didn't want to have to tell her whatever Theo expected him to, and he'd

called her mother a bitch and told Theo to go to
hell, and he had no right to say those things. But
worse was a realisation that his restraint was born
out of not caring for her. He felt sorry for her, little
else.

'I don't want to have to tell you, but it seems
Theo wants it that way.'

'And Theo always gets his own way,' she gibed
back at him.

His eyes narrowed and darkened but he made no
reply. Zoe slid to the edge of the bed, put the brandy
glass back down on the tray, but Franc prevented
her from standing up by grasping her hand.

She felt the *frisson* in the touch, wished she
hadn't, but remarkably it was still there—her love
and need for a man who didn't care a goat's hair
for her.

'Don't run away, Zoe, because I'll only have to
run after you.'

'I wasn't going to run away,' she told him bravely.
'I was going to open the door for you to leave.'

'I'm going nowhere, Zoe. When I'm asked to do
something, I do it.'

She raised a cynical brow. 'Like the job, whatever
that may be, that Theo asked you to do.'

'The job was to keep you safe for a while.'

Zoe's cynically raised brow slid down to a frown
of suspicion. 'Meaning what?'

He was still holding her hand, and it softened as
his thumb ran over her burning flesh. 'Sit down
and I'll tell you.' He sighed. 'You won't like it, sweet
one——'

'Then I don't want to hear it if it comes with
your condescension and false sympathy. You're

right, I'm not a child, but you're wrong about me being lonely. I'm not and never have been. Where you got that idea from I'll never know.' She pulled her hand from his and rubbed it as if he had stung her.

'There's nothing to be ashamed of in being lonely, Zoe. It hits us all some time in our lives.'

Zoe let out a small cry of mirth. 'You'll be telling me next you suffer from it too. That I don't believe. Too many women in your life to fill any empty hours you might have.'

'Women don't fill my empty hours, but work does,' he told her coldly. 'But that isn't the issue here—your loneliness is. The more I come to think of it, that was the likely reason you were so eager for my love that night in Switzerland.'

She could tell by the tensing of his facial muscles that he wished he hadn't said that. For once her supposition was spot-on. He raised regretful smoke-grey eyes to hers. 'I'm sorry. That was uncalled for,' he offered tenderly.

'But true,' she told him in a whisper of desperation. 'You were the first man ever to want me.'

His eyes held hers and then he seemed to give himself a mental shake and looked away from her.

'Whatever the reasons, it's not really relevant now. I just wanted to stress a point to Theo that he seemed to have overlooked—that you are very vulnerable and you need him now, not me.'

If she needed anyone in her life it was Franc Blakemore and not her surrogate father, but neither of them would ever know that—neither of them cared enough.

'And why should I need anyone in my life, now or ever?' she asked flintily.

'Because everyone needs someone.' He looked up at her then. 'Theo should be sitting here now,' he told her earnestly. 'I told him it was his place, not mine——'

'To tell me what?'

'Why I'm here now, why I took you off to that island.'

'Does it need an explanation? I thought I knew all that.'

'Sweet one, you knew nothing.' There was a pause as he tried to find words, and when they came they were delivered coldly and almost bitterly. 'Theo hired me to take you away from here.'

The statement came so coldly to her ears that they buzzed tempestuously and the room tilted. She sank back down to the bed, her legs like jelly.

'Hired you?' she grazed with an enormous effort, her fists tightening in her lap. 'When? Now?'

He shook his head. 'Not now; that was an added request. After my job was over. Theo wanted you brought back here and then for me to stay with you till they got back. He originally hired me to take you to that island for your safety.'

'Safety?' she cried incredulously.

'Yes, sweet one, safety.'

'But I wasn't in any danger!' Zoe shook her head with confusion. She'd only taken one mouthful of brandy and yet all was suddenly fuzzy. 'It was you who was in danger,' she protested, 'running from some kidnapper or assassin. The cover-up, the mysterious trip to an unknown island, the para-chute jump, the...the gun. You did all that because you were in danger, not me. You told me that.'

'I told you nothing of the sort, Zoe. I never once directly admitted that it was I who was in danger.'

She recalled he hadn't. 'But you led me to believe——'

'For your own protection. You presumed as much and I let you believe it, but I didn't lie to you——'

'You . . . you skirted the truth.'

He studied her with smoky grey eyes that pleaded for understanding. 'Whatever I have done for you, Zoe, I did with caring in my heart.'

She couldn't appreciate that. There was too much confusion and disbelief rattling around inside her, and it seemed to freeze the words in her throat.

'You...you say danger...but I'm not in danger. I've never been in danger.'

'You were, Zoe, but not any more. You're safe now and you have nothing to fear.' He reached out and took her hand to comfort her, rubbing his thumb across the back of her hand. 'A threat was made against you——'

'A threat?' Zoe cried, pulling her hand away. 'No one has need to threaten me. I'm no one.' Her mind pulsed furiously. Had some crazed person believed her to be the daughter of Theo, threatened to take her hostage, to hold her for ransom for some enormous slice of Theo's wealth?

'You're someone pretty important to a lot of dangerous people,' Franc told her gravely.

His voice was so softly timbred and so deadly serious that Zoe's heart started to throb painfully.

She began to feel the danger now even though Franc had assured her it had passed.

'Tell me, Franc,' she whispered, her dark eyes wide with concern. 'I need to know.'

It was then that Franc stood up and moved across the room, taking up a position by the balcony doors. Zoe was aware of his discomfort as if what he had to tell her he couldn't face himself. She had called him a coward and suddenly she knew that to be true. It angered her, and she went to his side and pulled him to face her.

'Tell me!' she cried. 'You said I wasn't a child, so why do you treat me like one?'

His ragged sigh vied with the buzz of the cicadas outside, steeling Zoe's emotions to take the blow she knew he was preparing to deliver.

He lifted his head to look at her, his facial muscles strained. 'You say you're no one, but you are—you are the daughter of Leonard Marston.'

Leonard Marston! A name—the name of her father? She'd never heard of it before. No one, but *no one*, had ever mentioned him before, and now it had come from Franc. Was this what Theo had wanted Franc to do—to tell her who her father was? The hurt inside her swelled till she could hardly breathe. She partly understood Franc's reluctance. He was right. Theo and her mother should be here. It wasn't his place to tell her about her father.

'Does that name mean anything to you, Zoe?' Franc asked.

She shook her head and swept the hair that fell across her face away from her burning skin. 'The surname—it's mine,' she husked, 'but no. I've never

heard of him.' It was a horrible confession to make.
She'd never heard of her own father.

'He's been in the news lately.'

'News? I never hear anything that goes on in the
outside world. I live in a vacuum—Theo's vacuum,'
she murmured miserably. She braved herself to ask
the next question. 'Who is he—an actor, a writer?'

Franc turned from her then, went to the tray and
poured himself another brandy. Zoe watched him
silently and then her anger erupted. How dared he
keep moving away from her, evading her questions, driving her crazy like this?

'For God's sake tell me, Franc; who is my
father?'

He faced her, and she got the impression it took
an enormous strength of will to do it.

'An agent, a United Nations drugs investigator.'

Zoe took a sharp intake of breath. She hadn't
expected that.

'An Englishman by birth. Ex-Secret Service,'
Franc went on levelly. 'He joined the United
Nations Drugs squad ten years ago and has been
working in South America for the last five. Zoe,
are you all right?'

She wasn't. The blood had drained from her face
and she felt weak and sick. Franc came to her and
handed her the brandy, and now she understood
why he had brought it to her room. She took it
gratefully and took a sip to calm her insides.

'I'm all right now, go on.'

'Your father was devoted to his work. There was
no room in it for . . . for anyone.'

'My mother, me!' she blurted, her eyes already
filling with tears.

'His job wouldn't allow it, Zoe. A man like that wasn't allowed emotions.'

Like you! she wanted to cry, but didn't, because she was beginning to understand. Her heart cried for her mother but it also cried for herself. This Leonard Marston had had no time or inclination in his life to give his heart to her mother or acknowledge the birth of his daughter because of his work, and Franc Blakemore was the same. There was no room in his life for love, just a string of women for instant gratification and nothing else.

She braced herself. 'You sound as if you know him. Do you?'

'Not as a friend. Leonard Marston wasn't a man to allow friends into his life. I'd met him several times and he was an insular man. Cold, if you like.'

'You didn't like him?'

'I respected him.'

'Meaning you didn't like him,' Zoe persisted.

'Theo has been more a father to you than Leonard Marston could ever be.'

'And what is that supposed to mean?' she bit out. 'That I should forget my true father's existence? That I should be oh, so damned grateful for all that Theo has done for me?' She gulped at her brandy, hurt and in great pain for what her true father had deprived her of, but more, more than that, for what Franc Blakemore had taken from her. She swallowed hard.

'I . . . I don't understand what all this has to do with me now.'

'Your father and his team had spent years investigating the drug barons in South America. This year all his hard work came to fruition. They had a case for prosecution, and your father was the chief prosecution witness. The biggest drugs bust the world has ever known,' Franc told her.

Suddenly Zoe needed air. She stepped out on to her balcony and slumped down in a plaited cane chair. Franc joined her with the brandy bottle. He sat across from her, placing the bottle down on a glass-topped table between them.

'This is hard for you, Zoe, I know, and perhaps now you can understand my fury with Theo and your mother. It isn't my place to have to tell you about your father but . . . well, in the circumstances I feel a certain sympathy with them. They love you——'

'But not enough.' She let out a ragged sigh into the warm, balmy night air. 'You're right. They should be here.' She frowned. 'But there is more, isn't there?' She lifted her bowed head to look at him.

He nodded. 'Yes, much more, but if you're not ready for it——'

'I am. All this has something to do with your taking me away, hasn't it?'

Franc leaned back in his seat and cradled his brandy glass in his hands. 'The drugs world is vicious, Zoe, and powerful. Your father's work was dangerous. Perhaps you can excuse him for never acknowledging you. In a way it was for your own protection, but unfortunately even that wasn't enough to protect you in the end.'

Zoe's heart started to hammer. 'I don't under-stand . . .' She shook her head.

'The drug barons wanted to silence your father before the trial. They couldn't get to him personally, he was too well protected, but a month ago, in spite of the high security surrounding him, his apartment in Lima was broken into.' Franc gazed deeply into the golden brandy in his glass, now swirling it around as if it might have the power to fire away what he wanted to say.

Zoe felt his tension in the warm night air and wanted to ease it for him because now she was beginning to understand the seriousness of what he was trying to tell her.

'Franc,' she uttered softly, 'go on. I have to hear it all.'

He raised his eyes from the glass and looked at her, so agonised that she wanted to rush to him, to offer him some sort of comfort.

He took a deep breath and looked away. 'In your father's apartment they found a photograph, a picture of a child. That child was you, Zoe. Many, many years ago your mother sent him a photo of the child he refused to acknowledge, probably in a desperate attempt to get him back. He kept that picture—not on his person, that was too risky, but in his apartment. It was all the drug barons needed because they knew that child must be special to him for him to have secreted it in his home. They set out to find you.'

Zoe couldn't breathe and heat scorched her throat but she could just utter enough to urge him on.

'Hostage?' she husked fearfully.

Franc nodded. 'Your father alerted the security forces working with him as soon as he realised the picture was missing. One of them was an old colleague of mine; we'd worked in the Middle East together and he knew I'd advised Theo in the past.

I immediately contacted Theo and...and the rest you know.'

'Me,' Zoe breathed hesitantly, already shaking her head in disbelief. 'It was me who was in danger, not you. Oh, my God!' She lowered her head and cradled it in her hands.

Franc came to her then, crouched down beside her and lifted her head. He smoothed his warm hands down the side of her face. 'I'm sorry, my darling, truly sorry that it's necessary to tell you all this.'

Zoe grasped his arms, not to push him away but for support. All her strength had gone, every last gram of it. 'Theo...kept me close to him this past year. He must have known...something like this would happen. I...I felt like a prisoner.'

'He's always felt protective towards you because he's always known who your father was. He could never have anticipated this, not the extent of it, but it was always a possibility. He gave your mother security and you too, because he loves you both. Heraklea made a big mistake in her life and you were the result, but Theo was there for you both.'

There was silence between them as Zoe digested that. At last she spoke. 'And my mother...she made another mistake...sending my father a...a picture of me.' Oh, God, her poor mother, knowing she had unwittingly exposed her daughter to such danger. No wonder she wasn't here—she couldn't face her.

Slowly Zoe let her trembling hands drop from his arms. She leaned back in her seat and stared beyond him to the black sky and the stars.

'So…so you were hired to protect me?' she asked in a faint whisper.

His reply took forever to come. 'Yes,' he said quietly. 'Theo hired me to keep you safe, to take you to a safe haven. He knew of the island and I made the security arrangements to get you away from here. Hence the secrecy, the unconventional mode of travel, even the mild sedation en route. If you had any suspicions that you were a target you might have unwittingly blown our cover.'

All the life drained from her, leaving her weak and barely conscious, but her mind spun unwillingly. It spun thoughts of the pain her mother must be suffering, of Theo's protection over the years around in her brain till she felt sick with trauma. But there was a worse thought that urged for space, and she hated herself for allowing it to strengthen because it was a totally selfish thought. Franc had simply been doing a job in taking her away. And had his lovemaking been part of that job too or was he just an opportunist, taking what was on loan as before? She closed her eyes and clenched her fists on the arms of the chair. He was even here now against his will, the job not over yet. Just around to keep an eye on her till Theo and her mother returned.

She found the strength to open her eyes and mouthed a few words, strange words that didn't seem to come from her own thoughts but were put there by an unknown force. 'You can go now. I don't need you here, Franc Blakemore. As you so rightly said I'm not a child any more. I can look after myself. I'm all I've got.'

'I'm not leaving, Zoe,' he told her calmly, 'because it isn't finished yet.'

'No, of course, you haven't been paid yet——'

'And stop that,' he grated.

She gave him a thin smile. 'It's true, isn't it? You didn't do this for nothing. You're just hanging around for your pay cheque——'

'Stop it!' he ordered. He stood up and raked his hair from his brow, and Zoe watched him; the look of sheer exhaustion on his face speared regret through her senses. He'd done his best for her for whatever monetary reasons.

'I'm sorry,' she murmured, kneading her forehead with trembling fingers. 'I don't know why I'm doing this, saying these awful things. It's all been such a shock.' Shakily she got to her feet. 'I really do want to be on my own now. I want you to go.'

She went to move past him but he reached out for her. She tensed as his hand locked around her wrist. 'I can't leave you yet.'

Those few words came gratingly and her nerves were instantly on alert. He'd said it wasn't finished yet.

'The trial—it isn't over yet?' she murmured, her heart filling with a new fear. Surely she wasn't still in danger? 'Back at the island...you said the danger was over...' Her voice trailed away because she didn't understand.

It was then he reached for her and folded his arms around her. He held her feverish, trembling body close to his, smoothing a hand over her silken hair, soothing her.

'Franc, what is it?' she whispered dully against his shoulder.

'Dear God, this is what I didn't want to have to do.' Slowly he drew back from her and cupped her flushed face in his hands, looking deeply into her widened eyes. 'The trial isn't for another month——'

Her heart constricted. 'So...so I'm still at risk?' she husked. With Franc as her protector she had no fear for her life, but her sanity was in great danger. She had suffered so badly loving him on that island, and now her agony was going to go on for another month. Four weeks of loving him...for nothing at the end of it.

'There is no danger for you now, only sadness.' He took a deep ragged breath. 'I did my job too well, Zoe. They...they never found you, but yesterday...yesterday your father was assassinated in South America——'

Her fevered scream of protest rose in the warm night, hung suspended in the air and then crashed around her ears till she screamed again and again.

'My darling, I'm so very sorry,' Franc grated, and took a firmer grip on her as she struggled to be free.

'Oh, God, no...' she cried frantically.

She went limp in his arms, a deep, deep rush of blood misting her mind feverishly. In an instant thoughts of her mother, of Theo, of the terrible, terrible job they had left Franc to do swam crazily in and out of her head till she didn't know where or who she was.

She felt Franc lift her and lay her on the bed, and the room swam.

She was only vaguely aware of him bathing her forehead as she moaned incoherently. Gradually he eased her clothes from her body. She wanted to cry but no tears would come and she didn't know why. You couldn't grieve for a father you hadn't known and yet there was a despair and a fury and a great, great sadness.

'Don't leave me,' she husked as he eased a fine cotton sheet over her body. Her arms came up and clung round his neck because she needed him—oh, so badly.

'I won't leave you,' he murmured, and lay down next to her on the bed. He cradled her in his arms, holding her to him as if she were a child. Her heart cried out for her father, her mother and for Theo, but though she despised herself for her selfishness her heart cried desperately for herself. It contracted painfully in despair for something she couldn't have but so desperately wanted: the love of the man who was comforting her now because he had been paid to do it.

CHAPTER NINE

FRANC was still with her when she awoke in the small hours still dressed in suffocatingly hot jeans and a very crumpled white short-sleeved shirt. He was asleep but not relaxed. She was sure of that.

She trailed a hot finger down his golden arm, and her thoughts began to clear but gave her no satisfaction. Biting her lip to stem a fresh wave of pain in her heart, she tried to sleep again because if she didn't it would hurt too much to think.

The sun was high when she came out of her stupor. She was alone. Very slowly she got up. Her head was thick and painful and she groped to the bathroom to rinse her face. The mirror over the sink effectively reflected her distress. She had no colour; the shock of Franc's revelations had drained the sun of the island from her skin. Her eyes were puffed and very dark, her lips swollen as if she had bitten them through the night.

She slipped on a cool cotton dress and went to the balcony. Franc was swimming in the pool below, taking long, powerful strokes through the water, on and on as if trying to ease the ache of his burden from his body and soul. The burden of herself.

She felt so desperately sorry for him. His job hadn't been a pleasant one. He'd been hired to protect the daughter of Leonard Marston and then hired to tell her he was dead. Her father was dead. She had never known him and he had never known her and the only emotion she could bring to her fevered senses was one of deep, deep sadness, not grief. Her mother would be devastated and that was why Theo had taken her away. She realised now how deeply Theo had cared for Heraklea over the years. That was some small comfort. Her mother had someone, Zoe Marston had no one.

She went down to the kitchen she barely had need to frequent and made coffee and poured orange juice. She took the laden tray out to the terrace by the pool, sat down under a shady umbrella and waited for Franc to finish his marathon swim.

He didn't see her and finally pulled himself from the pool and went to the changing-rooms. When he came out in shorts and vest-top, rubbing his hair with a towel, he saw her and joined her without a smile.

'How do you feel this morning?' he asked.

'How do you?'

He sat down and Zoe poured two coffees. 'I don't matter,' he replied. 'You're the one who matters.'

Zoe sighed. 'I think it was worse for you. You had an awful job to do and it couldn't have been pleasant.' He said nothing but continued to rub at his hair, and Zoe watched him, her heart expanding with her love. He hadn't asked for all this; it had been forced on him. 'I'm sorry you had to do it. It was unfair of Theo to expect so much; after all, a job is a job and——'

'Please don't, Zoe,' he murmured at last, draping the towel over a spare chair to dry in the sun. 'It's over with now but I'm still concerned for you.'

'You're concerned because you're paid to be.' She bit her tongue as soon as that was out. His eyes darkened but he made no reply, which made her feel worse.

'I'm sorry, I shouldn't have said that; it was out of order.' He nodded his acceptance of her apology and Zoe went on, 'I'm all right.' She clutched her coffee-cup and knew that she was; there was no alternative than to be all right. 'I feel sad that he's dead . . .' She stopped. He didn't want to hear this. He just wanted to know that she could cope without him and then he would be off to his next assignment, possibly his last if all he had told her was true.

'Go on,' he murmured, leaning back in his seat.

'About what?'

'You must talk it out, Zoe, otherwise it will knot you up.'

'Another of your instructions from Theo—group therapy before you leave?'

'You have the makings of a bitch,' he remarked as he leaned forward to pick up his coffee.

'I thought I already was one.'

'I've never said that,' he reminded her.

'Only by implication. It's enough.'

'Since when have you known what ticks in my mind?'

'Since when have I ever known *anything* about you?' she retorted.

He stared painfully at her and she looked away. This was ridiculous, she thought fretfully.

'Fighting isn't getting us anywhere,' she said, helping herself to more coffee.

'It could be beneficial.' He held out his coffee-cup for her to refill it, which she did. 'At least it's getting rid of your pent-up feelings.'

'I haven't got any,' she retorted.

'You're riddled with them, Zoe.'

'You make it sound like a bad case of terminal woodworm.'

He smiled wryly. 'A very apt description, I'd say. Strangled emotions can eat away at your psyche till there's little left but sawdust, then you're in trouble, not a leg to stand on.'

'Well, I'm not a piece of Chippendale, thank you. I'm flesh and blood and my emotions are just fine, and I don't need you to shove them around where they don't want to go.'

'In that case we'll pass our time together the way we did on the island.'

Her heart seized. 'You bastard! I wondered how long it would be before you brought that up. It's the one thing I do know about you—your crippling sex drive. Sex with a capital S!'

'The S goes for Scrabble, remember?'

'Oh, I remember all right!' she blurted furiously. 'There's nothing wrong with the functioning of my memory banks.'

'Nothing wrong with the functioning of your hormones, either. They matched mine and over-rode them at times too.'

Her anger and pain engulfed her. Her coffee-cup narrowly missed his head, but there was more. Fury shot her to her feet and defence shot Franc Blakemore to his. He caught her wrists to stem the blows she wanted to inflict on him, the physical hurt she wanted to shower on him.

'Easy, Zoe, nothing . . . comes out of vi-olence . . . only this.'

His mouth crashed against hers, hot and punishing. She had no chance to avoid it but the power of his lips only had the effect of rushing more anger and hurt to her senses. She suffered the kiss only long enough to get those crazed senses into some order of sanity then, with a renewed strength, she tore her mouth from his.

'I hate you, Franc Blakemore!' she screamed violently.

'Good,' he grazed darkly, his grip tightening and shaking her. 'Now more, Zoe. I want more than just that.'

She was trembling with rage, every pulse in her body wanting to hurt and hurt more.

'I know just what you want!' she cried bitterly. 'You...you want what you wanted that...that night in Switzerland—a body, any body! Whatever was on offer! You...you take...just take...nothing more. My father...my father is dead and...and Theo isn't here...no one is here for me.'

'I'm here for you, Zoe.'

'Liar!'

With one last effort she was free from him and running so hard that it hurt, her legs somehow finding the strength to spur her away from him. She reached the rock on the beach. Her rock where she had found solace so often in her life. She collapsed against it, pounding her fists on it, out of sight of the villa and the world, and then she burst into tears—the first flood of tears that would wash away the pain of life. Except it didn't; it just made her feel worse and worse till she crumbled in a heap on the sand and wanted to die.

Suddenly his arms were around her, pulling her hard against his chest.

'My poor darling. I'm sorry, sweet one. Cry and cry and get it all out.'

She knew then, as she sobbed helplessly against his chest, that he had pushed her, wound her to breaking-point, to release the pain and the anguish. She knew, but didn't understand why he felt the need to take that on his shoulders. The tears went on and on.

He held her for what seemed like hours, smoothing his hand over her hair, sometimes grazing soothing kisses over her brow. She clung to him and let him comfort her till at last there were no more tears.

'You...you did it on purpose, didn't you? Pushed me over the edge till I fell.' She tried to push away from him but he held on, only shifting his position to lean back on the rock to hold her in his arms more comfortably.

'You needed pushing, Zoe. You didn't cry last night and you should have done. You can't harbour all that grief and pain inside you. It does more harm in than out.'

'But...but I don't feel grief,' she tried to explain. 'I mean, I do, but not the normal sort of grief. I didn't know him. I didn't know what he looked like or how old he was or anything about him at all.'

'But you feel cheated, don't you?'

She let out a ragged sigh. 'Yes, you're right. I shouldn't, I know, but I feel...sort of angry and raw inside.'

'Angry with Theo and your mother?'

She nodded. 'I suppose so. Years ago, when I was old enough to realise there was a father missing in my life, I asked my mother, but she went into a fury and wouldn't talk about him. Theo just told me the barest of details—that he was English and didn't want to know. She's spent all her life waiting for a man who obviously didn't care enough about her.'

She bit back the irony of that. Without really knowing it she herself had in fact been waiting three years for the man she loved to walk back into her life. He had, and it had brought her nothing but grief, but perhaps she was more fortunate than her mother—at least she knew that Franc didn't want her, whereas her mother had never known for sure. She had just lived every day with hope in her heart.

'Maybe it would be kinder to think that he did love her and wanted to love you too,' Franc suggested. 'Don't forget he kept your picture. That was acknowledgement enough that he accepted you as his daughter, and in the end he did everything in his power to protect you. Your mother must know that and draw some small comfort from it. Circumstances wouldn't allow him a normal life. His work was very demanding and he was always at great risk himself; a wife and daughter would have added to his constant anxiety. Maybe he loved her too much but was doing her a kindness with his rejection.'

'Saving her life, you mean?' she murmured desolately. Slowly Zoe's heart began to thud. Maybe Franc, for that very same reason, wouldn't allow his heart to rest with anyone even if he cared deeply enough. Maybe he cared for her . . . but couldn't acknowledge it. But no . . . she was dreaming, hoping, looking for some small straw to clutch at.

'That is something we will never know for sure,' Franc suggested quietly.

'It's not knowing that's so heart-breaking. Someone dies and carries their emotions to the grave and leaves behind that terrible doubt. My mother will have to live with that—not knowing anything for sure.'

'I think she must know that he did care for her, otherwise why keep your picture? That must be some comfort to her. She has Theo to help her through, as she's had him to help her through all those lonely years of waiting.'

But I have no one, Zoe thought hopelessly, though at this moment in time Franc was still with her. But he would be going soon and then what?

'Has Theo loved her all these years?' she asked. She sensed that he and Theo were close and he would know. She remembered their embrace that day they had left the villa to go to the island with no name. Greek men often embraced but Franc wasn't Greek so it meant there was a strong bond between them.

'Theo keeps his emotions close to his heart. You must know that but, yes, she's always been very special to him and hopefully he'll pull her out of this——'

'And marry her and live happily ever after,' she interrupted morosely. 'Am I too old to be adopted by Theo, do you think?'

Franc laughed and hugged her tighter to him. 'Far too old,' he teased. 'But you don't need to be adopted to realise how much he cares for you.'

Zoe sighed. 'Yes, I see a lot of things now. He's always done the very best for me but I was always too spoilt and selfish to understand it. I suppose I was the daughter Heraklea denied him. He could easily have hated me and her for that, but he didn't. He looked after us both.'

'He was distraught when he found out that your life had been threatened.'

'He didn't show it, just ordered me to do as I was told as if I were a child again.'

'If he'd shown those emotions it would have done more harm than good. If he'd been honest with you it would have terrified you. That's why we concocted that story about my needing your secretarial services,' Franc explained.

'Yes, of course,' Zoe murmured, understanding now. 'I thought I was out on loan again, as you thought I was on loan that night three years ago.' And like a fool she had thought Franc had especially asked for her; like a fool she had thought he really wanted her—but it had all been an unsatisfactory dream. Oh, yes, he had wanted her, bodily but not spiritually. And she had given all and received nothing in return, and that was just as her mother had done; and that was a very painful thought.

Franc had no comment to make about her being on loan and she didn't push it because there was nothing to push for. She lay in his arms staring out across the shimmering blue sea, and thought how sad and ironic life could be.

'Why did you call my mother a selfish bitch?'

Franc sighed. 'I shouldn't have been so harsh with Theo. I regret it now and I wish you hadn't heard it. I was angry with them both for not being here for you when I brought you back. I didn't want to have to tell you about your father; I thought it was your mother's place to do that. I still think she was selfish all those years to deny you the love you needed. But an obsession can do that to you—turn you into yourself with no thought for others.'

'She must have loved him very much.' Zoe knew and understood now, but she also knew she was different. If she was carrying Franc's child, that child would be the centre of her universe.

'Franc,' she murmured after a reflective pause. 'You said my father was chief prosecution witness in this drugs trial; does that mean that those people will now go free because he's dead?'

'Your father would have anticipated an assassination attempt and covered himself. Though he was the main power he worked with a team and they will carry on without him. He was a brilliant man, totally dedicated to destroying the drug world. The trial will go on and hopefully justice will be done. Think of your father as a hero, Zoe, because he gave his life for what he believed in.'

As she lay in Franc's arms she reflected on all he had said and her heart went out to the father she had never known, and to her mother who had waited in hope, and to Theo for being there for everyone.

'Do you feel better now?' he asked at last. They had lain in the sand for a long, long time, Zoe silently wringing out her emotions and coming to terms with them, Franc holding her, smoothing her hair and just waiting patiently.

'Yes,' she answered calmly, and it was the truth. 'Where are they, Theo and my mother?' She eased herself out of his arms. He'd done his duty and she really ought to be pulling herself together, though she knew in her heart it would take a long, long time.

They both stood up and brushed sand from their clothes.

'South America. Your mother wanted to pay her last respects.'

'Painful for Theo,' Zoe said unhappily.

'A pain he is happy to endure if there is joy and happiness to follow.'

Zoe's eyes flickered uncertainly at that. 'A very profound thought,' she murmured, refusing to meet his grey eyes.

He lifted her chin to look into her reluctant eyes. 'A pain many of us are willing to endure, if the truth be known.'

He lowered his mouth to hers and Zoe had no chance to reflect on that cool remark. For one, she didn't understand it; for two, the contact of his warm lips dulled everything from her mind. The kiss was long and so very bitter-sweet. It encapsulated all that had happened between them, it reflected the heat and the passion of their days on that mystical island, the sun and the moon and the stars. It raised her hopes and dashed them equally smartly. It could be a goodbye or a start to something she so longed for—a life with the man she loved.

Her arms came up and folded around his neck; she wondered how he would interpret it and prayed he would take it for what it was—her love. But she

had given so much and said so much before, and
still he hadn't made that longed-for commitment.
Her heart for his.

He held her hard against him and she felt the
pressure of his desire, but it was no consolation to
know she had the power to arouse him so swiftly
and so devastatingly easily. For him it was a reflex
reaction, motivated by senses he had no control over
and had little to do with love. She felt the same
power pulsing deep inside her, the need for that
heady physical contact, and though the desire was
there it was tempered with hopelessness—a severe
dragging feeling of despair and longing for something that was unobtainable.

She eased the pressure of her arms and her lips,
tried to step back from him, but he held her firmly,
bringing one hand up to her chin to prevent her
from looking away from him.

She was forced to look directly into his eyes and
she didn't like what she saw—anger and disbelief
that she should reject him so.

'Don't look at me that way,' she uttered coldly.

'My God, I don't believe you,' he grated huskily.
'Just when I thought the pressure was off——'

'Just when you thought I was weak enough for
you to pounce!' she hit back sharply, her eyes filling
with fresh tears but held back by the anger that
flamed so easily against him. 'How clever you think
you are, offering me comfort and a shoulder to cry
on and then, when I'm exorcised——'

'Stop that, Zoe; are you so very blind, the way
your mother has been all these years?'

Zoe's eyes widened and she forced a cynical smile
to her lips. 'Blind to what?'

'To love, sweet one...' For a moment her heart raced uncertainly. 'Theo has loved her all these years but she couldn't see it.'

Zoe's eyes narrowed and her heart fluttered back to life. She couldn't speak, there was such a raw constriction in her throat. What was he saying? That he loved her, as Theo loved her mother? But those weren't the words she wanted to hear, using her mother and Theo as an example. She hesitated, too long, and clarification of his statement that she needed so urgently never came to fruition.

Franc's hands dropped to his sides. 'Ease up, Zoe, open your heart, because if you go on like this there will be no heart left for... for any man.'

She understood then. This wasn't about him and her; it was just an airy-fairy way of pressing home a point. 'Meaning you expect me to fall into your bed again?' she spiked at him.

His eyes darkened comtemptuously. 'I meant nothing of the sort. If you weren't so brittle and terrified of losing that beautiful face of yours you'd know exactly what I mean.'

'I only know what I know, Franc Blakemore,' she grazed levelly. 'That you think all my problems will be solved if I loosen up with you, as if you have the power to... to somehow get me back on my feet or, more to the point, back on my back!'

Oh, God, what was she saying? It was all going terribly wrong. Despair flooded her as he turned abruptly away from her, his face dark with rage, his shoulders so stiff that they were in danger of staying that way forever. She watched him stride off across the beach, not heading back to the villa but as far from her as was possible.

She knew she should run after him, to retract her terrible accusations, but it was hopelessly too late. She raised her eyes to the pale sky and blinked away tears she thought she had spent.

Two people could live their lives in this villa and never meet, she pondered as she swam her tenth length of the pool later that afternoon. He'd come back eventually, and made lunch for himself, made some phone calls and then gone out again. She hadn't seen him do all those things but all the signs were there to read: a discarded plate of salad in the kitchen, scribblings on Theo's desk pad by the phone, Theo's car gone from the garage. She tried to be angry about his taking the car. It wasn't his to take, but who knew what bargains the two of them had struck? After all, Franc Blakemore was on hire and she didn't know the terms.

She hauled herself from the pool, showered and slipped on a beach-wrap and was on her way up to her room to lie down in the cool—it was too hot outside—when she noticed a note by the phone on the hall table.

It was from Franc, giving her the telephone number of a hotel in Lima, Peru, where Theo and her mother could be contacted. Short and to the point, the note even included a suggested time to make the call.

Zoe glanced across at the grandfather clock. Half an hour to go; half an hour to decide what to say, to offer her condolences, to lie and say that she was coping when she wasn't . . .

She waited in the study, watching the clock, and when eventually she picked up the phone her hands were hot and trembling.

To her horror she burst out crying when she heard Theo's voice. She had wanted to sound strong, for everyone's sake, but she'd been through too much.

'Dear child,' Theo soothed down the phone, halfway across the world and a million miles away. 'Franc's obviously told you the whole story, but don't distress yourself any more, Zoe. It's all over now. Your mother is coping well but it's been a terrible time for us all and we must cope as best we can.'

Zoe fought for control and swallowed hard. 'Theo, I'm so sorry... for you and mother... No, don't wake her; let her sleep. Just give her my love.'

'Is Franc there with you?' Theo asked with concern deepening his voice.

She couldn't lie about that; he might want to speak to him. 'No, he's out at the moment...'

'Down at the offices on the marina, no doubt. I knew he'd be an asset to the company in spite of that temper of his. Tell him to call me when he gets back; I've some things to go over with him.'

Zoe's head reeled. 'What company, Theo? What are you talking about?'

'Koriakis Shipping, of course.' There was a small pause and then, 'He hasn't told you...? Well, that's understandable. I've asked rather a lot of him lately... But it's no secret that he's joining the company...'

Zoe's head stopped reeling but it was no relief. Her mouth opened and closed idiotically. Franc

Blakemore working for Theo? It didn't bear thinking about.

'I...I didn't know,' she murmured.

There was a chuckle from Theo. 'I expect he was keeping it as a surprise for you, and now I've spoilt it; never mind, I expect you two have had more important things on your mind. In spite of everything else, are you happy, Zoe?'

Happy? What a strange question...why should she be happy? Slowly her mind started to function as if it had been...blinded...yes, that was the word... But no, surely not?

'Theo?' she husked. Suddenly she was nervous, trembling all over. She didn't know how to put it, to ask what she was afraid to ask Franc. But she couldn't ask Theo directly; it would have to be done subtly. Frantically she went through her memory banks and found what she sought. 'You...you remember the day I left with Franc to...to go to the island?'

Suddenly Theo was serious. 'It's a day I'll never forget, Zoe, dear one. We were so very concerned for your life. You must forgive us for our actions but it was the only way to get you to safety——'

'I know,' Zoe interjected, 'it's not that. I understand now. You've always done the best for me, but it's something else I must know.' She took a deep breath because this was so very important to her life and she didn't want to make a mistake and get it all wrong. 'You said...you said a woman had eluded you and you looked no further——'

'Your mother, Zoe,' Theo told her gravely. 'I've waited for so long for her...' His voice trailed off, as if the final release was too much to talk about.

'I guessed that,' Zoe told him softly, 'and Theo, I know it's too soon after all that has happened, but I'm so very happy for you both.'

'You don't sound too happy——'

'Oh, I am,' Zoe insisted, forcing lightness to her voice to dispel any doubts he might have. 'It's just that . . . you said something about Franc . . . that he didn't look any further either. I . . . I was just curious to know what you meant.'

Zoe could hear the relaxation in his voice as he spoke the next words that seared hope to her heart. 'Why should he look further when he had you in his heart?'

Zoe laughed with him and the lightness in her heart and voice was real this time. So Theo knew— knew what she had been blind to. There was so much else she wanted to ask him, but it wasn't his place to tell her. It was Franc's, and now she wasn't afraid any more because she had something certain to build on.

She sent all her love to her mother and said that she hoped to see them soon, and her hands were still trembling when she put the phone down as they had been when she had picked it up—but for so many different reasons.

Where was it—that damned, wretched, wonderful, black silk dress?

For three years she had kept it somewhere here in this vast wardrobe—the dress Franc had so expertly slid from her eager body that night. She searched feverishly for it, her fingers sliding past silk and satin and designer labels by the score. She let out a small cry as she found it and hauled it out to hug it to her face.

The sun had set and the velvet cloak of darkness was swiftly settling around the silent villa. Franc wasn't back yet but she knew he would eventually return—not because he was paid to but because he would want to.

She bathed and brushed out her long, silky jet hair and added colour to her lips and eyes before stepping into the dress. Her new happiness was reflected in the brightness of her eyes, the glow of her radiant skin, the gleam of her hair; Franc wouldn't see any of that, but he would know it, he would feel it.

She went to his room, having already checked that it was the right one, though with no fear of her making a mistake this time, because he was the only house guest. What a terrible, wonderful mistake she had made in Switzerland. A shudder crawled up her back at the thought of what would have happened to her life if she hadn't made that error.

She waited by the window in the darkness, this time with a growing excitement that far outweighed what she had felt before. She gazed out over the pool area, watching the shadows dance as a light, warm breeze fluttered the scented oleanders. She heard the cicadas, then the purr of Theo's car and then her heartbeat.

At last the door opened, bathing her in golden light from the candle lamps outside in the corridor. She knew he had seen her, and thought she heard a soft intake of breath. Softly he closed the door behind him, shutting off the light; softly he came towards her.

Zoe felt the warmth of his presence, the same heady, musky scent that was his and his alone. He reached for her, smoothed the back of his hand down the side of her face.

She spoke to him, in Greek, a soft murmur she knew he would understand. His thumb brushed the words from her lips.

'And I love you too, my darling sweet one,' he husked, 'and what a wonderful feeling of *déjà vu.*'

She laughed softly and he placed his lips over hers to still them, his arms wrapping around her as if never to let her be free.

The kiss said it all as all his other kisses had done, but she had been blind and stupid and a little crazy not to have known. His hand slid to the front of her dress and his kiss turned to a smile on her lips.

'The same dress too. I'd have known its texture anywhere. Smooth silk, as lustrous and as sexy as its wearer. It's haunted me, Zoe; all these years it has haunted me. You, the night, I couldn't forget.'

'Nor I,' she murmured throatily, tracing her fingers over his face. 'I meant it, you know, my Greek love incantation. I didn't know you but I loved you. Isn't that crazy?'

'Crazy,' he agreed, 'but I was just as crazy and incensed when you weren't there the next morning. I thought——'

This time her fingers on his lips stilled him. 'I know what you thought—that I was on loan, but... but you still came back, though it took you three years to do it, and you wouldn't have done if...if...' She couldn't finish because the fate that

had brought them together again was too terrible
to mention.

'But I would have done, Zoe,' he grated painfully, knowing what she was thinking. 'I'd suffered
three years of indecision, wondering if that night
had meant as much to you as it had to me. The
words you spoke in the height of our lovemaking
haunted me too. I wanted to believe that they were
true, but we were strangers and I wasn't sure.'

'You were never sure of my love, were you?' she
whispered.

She felt his smile rather than saw it in the
moonless night. 'You told me as I made love to you
that first time, and people say strange things in the
throes of passion, and then the other time you were
sedated and not in your right mind; then on the
island, though we made love, we never talked of
it,' he said.

'You talked of your love to Theo, though,' she
teased, running her fingers lightly through his hair.

His hands tightened around her waist. 'I wanted
him to know how deeply I cared for you—that I
would keep you safe and it was more than a job,
and when we came through it I hoped to marry
you.'

A small, soft gasp caught in her throat. 'You
didn't tell him about Switzerland?'

'Heaven forbid,' he laughed softly. 'A legend I
might be, but have no desire to be a dead one. I
admitted to Theo that I had fallen in love with you
at his birthday party the night before. Love at first
sight, I pleaded, and it must have appealed to his
romantic Greek nature because he accepted it
without question; but in a way it was true, though

three years spanned in between. Have no fear, my darling; Switzerland is our secret.'

'A wonderful secret,' she murmured as his hand caressed her back and drew her ever closer to him till she felt that wonderful need power between them.

'I loved you that night, my sweet one, with my body and my heart. I thought I loved my work but it soured after that night. But I didn't know how you felt and I had business commitments, assignments I just couldn't walk away from, and it all took time. I wanted to be free of it all because until I was I couldn't offer you any security. I couldn't have carried on my work and loved you as well. I'd have lived in fear for your life, not my own, and that would have been too tough to bear.'

'So all that work we did on the island was for us, for our future?'

'For our love, but I couldn't tell you that because I was still unsure of you—but Zoe, everything I did for you was with love; you must always remember that.'

'I wish you had told me that before, Franc, because I was so awful to you. I didn't know or understand. I just thought you had used me, and our last morning on the island was the very worst of all——'

'Can't you begin to understand how I felt? I'd heard about your father and I knew what you would have to go through when you found out. My heart was aching for you, dying for you.'

Zoe pressed her warm mouth to the side of his cheek. 'Oh, my darling, I think you've suffered more than me. I promise I'll make it up to you. I promise I'll love you forever and tell you every day of our lives.'

'You can tell me now, the way you did the very first time.' His mouth closed over hers and she told him. Her lips told him, her warm, scented skin told him, her quickening breath told him.

Slowly—oh, so slowly—his hands slid her fine silk straps from her shoulders and he lowered his mouth to her naked skin. The feeling this time was more intense, more sensual than before because she knew he loved her. The knowledge excited her and spun her higher until she was desperate for him, clawing at her clothes to feel his hard flesh against hers.

'Steady, sweet one,' he warned. 'The night is going to be a long one.'

She laughed softly and sexily as he expertly dispensed with their clothes as he had done so expertly years before when she was on loan. But she wasn't on loan any more. She belonged to this man as she had never belonged to any man before.

With one feverish gesture he lifted her and carried her to the bed. They touched, they caressed, rediscovered every intimacy they had explored before and then when they could wait no longer he entered her and she cried out her love, drawing him into her till they moved and pulsed and adored each other as never before, onward and upward, till they reached the perimeters of that other strange world of mystic paradise that was theirs and theirs alone.

Later they lay exhausted in each other's arms, but the kisses didn't stop. It would be a long night, a long, sensuous night, Zoe thought dreamily, but it wouldn't end with her flight in the morning, because she wanted to be there when he awoke. She would be there every morning of his life to tell him how very much she loved him.

Next Month's Romances

Each month you can choose from a wide variety of romance with Mills & Boon. Below are the new titles to look out for next month, why not ask either Mills & Boon Reader Service or your Newsagent to reserve you a copy of the titles you want to buy — just tick the titles you would like and either post to Reader Service or take it to any Newsagent and ask them to order your books.

Please save me the following titles:	Please tick	√
HIGH RISK	Emma Darcy	
PAGAN SURRENDER	Robyn Donald	
YESTERDAY'S ECHOES	Penny Jordan	
PASSIONATE CAPTIVITY	Patricia Wilson	
LOVE OF MY HEART	Emma Richmond	
RELATIVE VALUES	Jessica Steele	
TRAIL OF LOVE	Amanda Browning	
THE SPANISH CONNECTION	Kay Thorpe	
SOMETHING MISSING	Kate Walker	
SOUTHERN PASSIONS	Sara Wood	
FORGIVE AND FORGET	Elizabeth Barnes	
YESTERDAY'S DREAMS	Margaret Mayo	
STORM OF PASSION	Jenny Cartwright	
MIDNIGHT STRANGER	Jessica Marchant	
WILDER'S WILDERNESS	Miriam Macgregor	
ONLY TWO CAN SHARE	Annabel Murray	

If you would like to order these books in addition to your regular subscription from Mills & Boon Reader Service please send £1.80 per title to: Mills & Boon Reader Service, Freepost, P.O. Box 236, Croydon, Surrey, CR9 9EL, quote your Subscriber No:................................. (If applicable) and complete the name and address details below. Alternatively, these books are available from many local Newsagents including W.H.Smith, J.Menzies, Martins and other paperback stockists from 14th May 1993.

Name:...

Address:...

....Post Code:........................

To Retailer: If you would like to stock M&B books please contact your regular book/magazine wholesaler for details.

You may be mailed with offers from other reputable companies as a result of this application. If you would rather not take advantage of these opportunities please tick box ☐

Another Face . . .
Another Identity . . .
Another Chance . . .

PENNY JORDAN

Silver

The international bestseller
from the author of *Power Play* and
The Hidden Years.

When her teenage love turns to hate, Geraldine Frances vows to even the score. After arranging her own "death", she embarks on a dramatic transformation emerging as *Silver,* a hauntingly beautiful and mysterious woman few men would be able to resist.

With a new face and a new identity, she is now ready to destroy the man responsible for her tragic past.

Silver – a life ruled by one all-consuming passion, is Penny Jordan at her very best.

W⬤RLDWIDE

YOURS FREE...
an exciting Mills & Boon Romance

Regular readers will know that from time to time Mills & Boon invite your opinions on our latest books, so that we can be sure of continuing to provide what you want - the very best in Romantic Fiction.

Please spare a few moments to tell us your views about the book you have just read and we will send you a FREE Mills & Boon Romance as our thank you.

Don't forget to fill in your name and address so we know where to send your FREE book!

Please tick the appropriate box for each question ☑

QUESTIONNAIRE

1 Did you enjoy reading LOVE ON LOAN by Natalie Fox?
Very much ❏   Quite a lot ❏   Not very much ❏   Not at all ❏

2 What did you like best about it?
The plot ❏   The hero ❏   The heroine ❏   The background ❏

3 What did you like least about it?
The plot ❏   The hero ❏   The heroine ❏   The background ❏

4 Do you have any comments you'd like to make about this book?

_____

_____

_____

5 Would you like to read other books of this kind?
Often ❏   Occasionally ❏   Never ❏

6 How many Mills & Boon Romances do you usually read in a month?
One or less ❏   2 to 4 ❏   5 to 10 ❏   More than 10 ❏

7 **Which of the following series of romantic fiction do you usually read?**

Mills & Boon: Romance ☐ Silhouette: Sensation ☐

Best Seller ☐ Special Edition ☐

Medical Romance ☐ Desire ☐

Temptation ☐

Duet ☐

Masquerade ☐

8 **From where did you obtain this book?**

Mills & Boon Reader Service ☐   New from the shops ☐

Other (please specify)

_____

9 **Are you a Reader Service subscriber?**   Yes ☐   No ☐

If yes, what is your subscription number?

_____

10 **What age group are you?**

16-24 ☐   25-34 ☐   35-44 ☐   45-54 ☐   55-64 ☐   65+ ☐

=== **THANK YOU FOR YOUR HELP** ===

Please send your completed questionnaire to:
MIlls & Boon Reader Service, FREEPOST, P.O. Box 236,
Croydon, Surrey CR9 9EL

NO STAMP NEEDED

Please fill in your name and address to receive your FREE book:

Ms/Mrs/Miss/Mr _____ EDLL

Address _____

_____

_____ Postcode _____